AT last Roseanna stepped onto the frozen surface. Flushed with excitement, she spun round and round on the same spot, like a top. By the time she stopped twirling in a circle, she was very giddy. She swayed and slithered about in an attempt to keep her balance.

She did not realize that she had gone too far until she halted to catch her breath. Then there was a resounding crack as the piece of ice on which she had been standing parted from the main body.

Roseanna screamed in terror. She could do nothing except stand erect and stare as the gap between the ice floe where she was and the Frost Fair grew wider and wider.

It was then she saw Count Czarski racing toward her.

Love in Exile

Blanche Chenier

FAWCETT COVENTRY • NEW YORK

LOVE IN EXILE

Published by Fawcett Coventry Books, a unit of CBS Publications, the Consumer Publishing Division of CBS Inc.

Copyright © 1980 by Blanche Chenier

ISBN: 0-449-50046-2

Printed in the United States of America

First Fawcett Coventry printing: May 1980

10 9 8 7 6 5 4 3 2 1

"I can't bear this any more!" Roseanna exclaimed.

"I agree," Evelina responded. "It is stifling."

"Oh, if only we could open the windows!"

"Amen!"

But they both knew that was impossible. If the windows were opened it would merely admit the sulphurous fumes, choking everyone to death.

"I have never known a fog to last so long!" Roseanna declared.

"Nor me either," Evelina replied.

For a week now, London and its suburbs had been shrouded in a deadly haze. There had been nothing like it since Cromwell's time.

Mrs. Poulet had insisted that the windows be kept tightly closed to prevent the raw vapors from entering. But this wise precaution created other problems. The smell of cooked food, of perfume, of burning coal, and of bleached washing lingered.

The close confinement forced on everyone by the

unhealthy atmosphere was taking its toll, and tempers were becoming frayed.

"It seems to have been here for all eternity!" Roseanna commented.

"Maybe it's starting to lift," Evelina suggested. "Have you looked out today?"

"Not yet," Roseanna answered.

She pulled back the shutters and pressed her nose against the steamed-up windowpane. The swirling clouds were still there, as thick and impenetrable as they had been since they first made their appearance on Boxing Day.

Roseanna sighed. She had experienced fog before, but never anything like this one. It was intolerable.

"Still there?" Evelina inquired.

"Yes, I must get out!" Roseanna cried.

"But..."

"I know. I know. But I can't stand being cooped up in the house any more. I have to go for a walk."

"But Roseanna, even if you take a stroll in the garden you may get lost."

That was the worst of this awful weather. The only people who could find their way were the blind. No one else ventured outside unless they absolutely had to.

"I realize that," Roseanna responded, "but I cannot endure it inside for another minute."

"Are you wise?" Evelina questioned. "What if you don't hear a carriage coming and you are knocked down?"

"There isn't any traffic," Roseanna reminded her.

Carriages had stopped traveling, since the coachmen could no longer see the road. One could almost touch the silence in North Row.

"So you are determined to leave the house," Evelina stated.

"Yes," Roseanna asserted.

"In that case, I'll come with you."

"Good."

They put on warm cloaks to protect themselves, and wrapped scarves around their faces to keep away the poisonous air, before stepping into the garden.

They knew that they were only a foot or two from

the house, but they might as well have been on another planet. They could discern neither the door they had closed behind them nor the gate in front of them.

Roseanna and Evelina clutched each other tightly, as if they were afraid they would be swallowed up in the menacing obscurity. Slowly and cautiously they inched along the path leading to the street. When at last their hands encountered the wooden gate which opened onto North Row, they heaved sighs of relief.

Then, suddenly, like a witch out of a seething caldron, an old woman emerged from the fog.

Roseanna and Evelina eyed the hag apprehensively. Who was she? What did she want?

"Mam'selle Poulet?" the old woman asked, speaking with a thick French accent.

Roseanna and Evelina stared at her. They were both "Mam'selle Poulet." So how should they answer her question?

The old woman seemed to divine their difficulty.

"Mam'selle Roseanna Poulet?" she clarified.

"C'est moi," Roseanna admitted.

"Parlez-vous français, mam'selle?" the old woman inquired.

"Oui," Roseanna replied.

"Good," the old woman continued in French. "A gentleman gave me a letter for you. He promised me one guinea for my trouble."

The woman extended her bony hands. The fingers of one of them rubbed together, indicating her desire for the money; those of the other held onto the epistle she had mentioned.

Roseanna and Evelina exchanged glances. Gentleman? What gentleman would write to Roseanna? Both girls were bewildered. They had no men friends. They were not even "out" yet. So who could the missive be from? And how had this ancient lady managed to find them?

"How . . . did you know . . . where to come?" Roseanna stammered in French.

"Your gentleman friend told me," the old woman returned.

7

"You don't live...in England...do you?" Evelina queried.

"No," was the terse response.

"Do you live in France?" Evelina persisted.

"That is my affair, I think!" the old woman exclaimed tartly. "You want this letter? Yes or no?"

"Yes! Yes!" Roseanna answered.

She was dying to discover whom it was from. Instinctively her hand stretched toward it, but the old woman snatched it out of reach.

"Money first—one guinea," she said. "Then you can have the letter. Be quick!"

Roseanna and Evelina fished about in their reticules. Neither of them possessed a whole golden guinea. However, between them they managed to raise the amount, with eight half-crown pieces and two sixpences.

The old woman surveyed the coins suspiciously. She counted them three times over before she agreed that they made up the correct sum. Then she thrust the letter into Roseanna's hand and disappeared into the murky mists from whence she had sprung.

Roseanna and Evelina, coughing even despite their protective scarves, hurried back into the safety and warmth of the house. They hung their cloaks up and quietly closed the door. After taking a drink of warm water to ease the rawness in their throats from the sulphur-laden atmosphere, they hurried to Roseanna's bedroom to read the note.

"I didn't know you had any beaux," Evelina teased when they were safe.

"Neither did I," Roseanna responded. "And I don't. This is my cousin Denis's scrawl. I'd recognize it anywhere."

"Your mama's nephew?" Evelina asked, unconsciously making the distinction between her aunt-by-marriage's relations and her own kin to Roseanna on their father's side. "The one who took us to see the illuminations of Vitoria?"

"The same."

"What ever is he doing sending messages to you through an old hag like that?"

Roseanna shrugged. "I have no idea," she answered, "but he is not one to play games."

"Hmmmm. Didn't I hear that he was employed by the Foreign Office?"

"Yes."

"What does he do there?"

"I'm not sure. He never talks about his work. I've always understood that there is something...well ...He is very secretive about it, at any rate."

"Perhaps he is in trouble."

"Perhaps," Roseanna returned, seating herself on the bed and opening the letter.

Evelina joined her.

"What does it say?" she asked.

"Wait a minute."

Roseanna frowned as she read, and then gasped.

"What is it?" Evelina questioned eagerly.

"He...he is writing from Craonne!" Roseanna cried.

"But...but that's in France!" Evelina exclaimed. "Isn't it?"

"That's right. This," Roseanna replied, indicating the paper in her hand, "has been smuggled to us."

"I don't believe it!"

They were at war with France. How could Denis Martin be there? It must be a joke!

"See for yourself," Roseanna exhorted.

Evelina leaned over Roseanna's shoulder. She could barely make out the address at the top of the letter, which was enough to confirm the truth of her cousin's words.

"But why? How did he get there? What ever possessed him to go?" Evelina demanded. "What does he say? Tell me! Tell me!"

"'My dear Roseanna,'" Roseanna read aloud. "'I have paid more than ten pounds—all I had on me—to have this letter brought to you—'"

"Ten pounds!" Evelina interrupted.

It was a huge sum of money. One could live on that for months. He must have been desperate, to have spent so much!

"He writes that he has been made a prisoner of the French," Roseanna explained.

"What! But that is terrible!"

Roseanna nodded in assent. "'I was on my way to join the British army in the south of France,'" she quoted from the letter, "'when I took the wrong turning and was captured.'"

"Bad luck," Evelina interposed. "Go on."

"'At first my imprisonment was tolerable,'" Roseanna deciphered. "'As an officer and a gentleman I was well treated. However, I learned this morning that the French army is coming past the château. I've seen these troops before. Undisciplined by their officers and embittered by the defeats they have suffered, they have a tendency to take revenge on whatever luckless prisoners fall into their hands. I don't want to sound alarmist, but I am afraid that unless I can escape from here I may be shot.'"

Roseanna stopped reading. "We must do something to help him!" she declared.

"We?" Evelina echoed.

"I can't do anything alone. You know that!" Roseanna cried. "Mama insists that we may not go anywhere on our own while we are not 'out,' and our coming-out party isn't until the end of the month."

"True, but even together, what can we do?" Evelina mused. Rush off to France to rescue him? "What does Denis suggest?"

Roseanna perused the missive once more. "He says we have to give this letter to his friend Count ..." She paused. "Oh, good heavens! I cannot read this word."

"Well don't ask me to," Evelina rejoined. "You're the only person I know of who is able to make sense of Denis's handwriting."

"We'll soon find out, I suppose," Roseanna remarked. "According to Denis, this Count Something-or-other is staying at his rooms in the Albany."

Evelina frowned. "In that case, why didn't Denis send him the letter direct?" she wondered.

"'For various reasons which I am unable to go into,'" Roseanna quoted, "'I felt my note had a better chance of reaching you in North Row than Count Something-or-other at the Albany. I'll try to tell you the reason when—and if—I return to England.'"

"Now," said Roseanna, "let's go to see this count, whoever he is."

"Very well," Evelina agreed.

The fog was still thick when the cousins ventured out of the house for the second time that day. However, though it presented quite an obstacle to them, Roseanna's determination to reach the Albany was enough to overcome the difficulties.

Roseanna led Evelina southeast, feeling her way along the once-familiar streets like a blind beggar. The pair of them avoided the vast wastelands of Hanover Square, Berkeley Square, and Grosvenor Square, where they might have become lost. Instead they chose to walk down narrow thoroughfares with plenty of shops, where the light from the windows was sufficient to guide them. Here, if they truly needed to, they could request further directions.

It seemed an eternity before they arrived at the Albany, where they were soon admitted. Nervously, Roseanna knocked on the door of her cousin's rooms. It was opened by a fashionably dressed man a few years older than herself, whose fair, slightly ruffled hair reminded her vaguely of a picture she had seen of the great composer Beethoven.

He stared at Roseanna and Evelina in astonishment.

"Ladies?" he inquired curiously, as if he imagined they had surely made a mistake and called at the wrong apartment.

Roseanna and Evelina curtsied. He returned their salutation with a bow.

"May we come in?" Evelina asked boldly.

"But of course," he answered, opening the door wide and ushering them into the sitting room. "But I am afraid Mr. Martin is not here at the moment."

Roseanna noticed that he had a faint accent, which she found attractive.

"I know," she replied.

"You . . . know?" their host echoed, surprised.

"Yes, we know," Evelina confirmed. "Allow us to

11

introduce ourselves. I am Evelina Poulet and this is my cousin Roseanna Poulet."

"I am Marek Anton Czarski," he responded. And then, almost as an afterthought: "Count Czarski."

"Oh, so that's how you pronóunce it!" Roseanna mused. "I wondered."

Count Czarski blinked. His eyebrows went up slightly. He appeared to be about to interrogate the cousins, then seemed to change his mind.

"Would you care for some tea?" he invited.

"Yes, please," Roseanna accepted with enthusiasm.

"That would be most welcome," Evelina agreed.

Especially after their unpleasant walk through the abrasive, raw, and stifling fog.

Count Czarski rang and a manservant entered the room. The count addressed him in a language the cousins did not understand. Then he scurried into the kitchen and returned in no time at all with a tray of things for tea.

Evelina, as senior lady present, poured.

As soon as everyone was served, Count Czarski turned to his guests.

"May I assist you in any way?" he inquired.

Roseanna suddenly realized that she had said nothing concerning the reason for their unorthodox visit.

"I am sorry," she apologized. "I should have explained, but...it is so difficult. I...we... well, we didn't know what to do about this...except bring it straight to you."

As she spoke, she handed him her cousin's letter, which he took from her and read, frowning.

"Denis must be in real trouble," he commented, "or he would not have considered asking *me* for assistance!"

"He sounds desperate," Roseanna said.

"He does rather," Evelina concurred.

"What neither of us understands is why he didn't write directly to you," Roseanna stated.

Count Czarski smiled. "Doubtless he did as he thought best," he answered enigmatically. "He trusts you both, I take it."

"Yes," Evelina replied before Roseanna could speak.

"Good. However, I must have your solemn promise

12

that you will not breathe a word of this to anyone," Count Czarski exhorted.

"You have it," Evelina vowed.

"We won't tell a soul," Roseanna assured him, "but..."

"Yes?" Count Czarski queried.

"Can you do anything to help Denis?" Roseanna asked anxiously.

Count Czarski smiled, making Roseanna feel as if she had been bathed in brilliant sunlight. Yet there was something in his expression which caused her to instinctively lower her eyes.

"I shall certainly try," the count responded.

Evelina frowned. "But what can you do?" she wondered. "How can you rescue Denis from Craonne?"

"You are a very inquisitive young lady," the count told her.

Evelina blushed. "I'm sorry," she said contritely, "but it does seem to me—"

"I don't think it would be wise for either of you to know my plans," Count Czarski cut in. "There is still a war on, and it might be dangerous—for all of us."

"I understand," Evelina murmured softly.

Roseanna shuddered. Somehow, without being explicit, Count Czarski had conveyed a sense of peril. Imminent and menacing. She could see the wild, undisciplined soldiers Denis had described brandishing their knives and firing their pistols indiscriminately...

"We...we didn't think of that," she commented.

"That is natural," the count remarked.

Here in England they had not had to experience the horrors of war. They had been sheltered from the realities of what was transpiring on the Continent. Of course they had news of the various battles. They might even have friends or neighbors who had lost their relatives in the fighting. But it wasn't the same as being in the front line of battle.

"Are you going to go to France?" Evelina questioned irrepressibly.

Count Czarski sighed.

"Oh..." Evelina had done it again. "Sorry."

She looked so comic, trying to appear abashed and

not quite succeeding, that Count Czarski could not but smile at her.

"Yes," he decided to reply, "and the sooner I leave, the better. But first, we shall escort the two of you home."

It did not occur to either Evelina or Roseanna to protest that as they had found their way to the Albany they could negotiate a route back to North Row. They submitted to Count Czarski's will in this matter with uncharacteristic meekness.

Together with his manservant Tomasz, Count Czarski accompanied the cousins through the still-foggy streets of London. Impulsively, as they reached the garden gate, Roseanna suggested that Count Czarski should come in and make the acquaintance of her mother.

"I must decline," Count Czarski returned.

"Oh? But why?" Evelina inquired. "Aunt would be delighted to meet you, and—"

"Denis told me you two were not 'out' yet," Count Czarski interrupted, "and I feel it would be better if you waited to introduce me to your family until you had entered society."

"Yes, you are right," Evelina agreed. "Good-bye, then."

"Good-bye," Count Czarski responded, kissing her fingertips.

Roseanna could not meet his eyes. "Good-bye," she murmured.

"Until we meet again," he returned, raising her hand to his lips.

Then he and his manservant disappeared into the mists.

"Well, that's that, then," Evelina stated as they closed the front door behind them and hung up their cloaks.

"What do you mean?" Roseanna queried.

"I was hoping for an adventure," Evelina replied, "but it seems that we have merely been postmen!"

"How disappointing for you," Roseanna commiserated.

"Do you think he'll manage to rescue Denis?"

"I don't know, but I had the impression he would do his best."

"I hope he isn't held up trying to cross the Channel," Evelina commented. "If he is..."

She left the rest of her sentence unspoken.

Roseanna knew what was on her cousin's mind. Time was of the utmost importance. If the French troops arrived in Craonne before Count Czarski... If the fog delayed the count... If he could not get to France ...If his plan didn't succeed... If the two of them, Denis and Count Czarski, were stopped as they fled...

"What's your opinion of him?" she inquired.

"Who?" Evelina countered.

"Lord Czarski," Roseanna clarified.

"He's nice... in a brotherly sort of way."

"Ye-e-es."

"What's the matter? Don't you like him?"

"Oh, yes."

"But?"

"I just don't feel...sisterly towards him."

"Oh," Evelina said. "Well, I do."

It was later, very much later, when Roseanna was in bed trying to go to sleep, that she tried to fathom why she had put it like that.

"If I don't feel sisterly towards him," she thought, "what do I feel?"

She recalled having tea with Count Czarski in Denis's sitting room. When he had looked at her, it had disturbed her. She had experienced a strange sensation...

"...rather like an egg that's beaten to a froth when it doesn't expect it," she reflected.

She had been all churned up inside. Yet it hadn't been unpleasant. And...

With a sudden pang she realized that she wanted to see him again, but she didn't know if that would be possible. He was going into danger. And there was no way of telling if he would survive.

"Come back to me!" Roseanna besought him silently. "Please come back to me."

2

The fog had gone. The day following Roseanna and Evelina's visit to the Albany, the wind had changed and it had lifted.

London had heaved a sigh of relief, but it was short-lived. The weather began to turn colder and colder and colder. Snowflakes started to fall.

At first, people had been intrigued by the novelty, but when the snow proceeded to descend for forty-eight hours without pause and the papers reported deaths caused by the freezing temperatures, their delight turned to horror.

Everyone declared that it was the iciest January within living memory, and that, coming so soon after the fog, it was not fair.

The entire country was covered with a sinister blanket of white. The roads were blocked, the mails were late, the ships retreated to the safety of their harbors. Each day people looked out at the scene and wondered when it would thaw; each day the skies were gray and more snowflakes tumbled down, adding to the drifts.

It snowed so seldom in London that few people had been provident enough to stock up on fuel. Mrs. Poulet was in the same boat as her neighbors. She had to use her supply of coal sparingly. Only two rooms in the house, the kitchen and the drawing room, were permitted to have fires; the rest of the house remained unheated.

Despite being warmly dressed, Roseanna and Evelina shivered frequently, and they decided to sleep together for warmth.

"I pity Aunt," Evelina commented. "Imagine having no one to share her bed! How cold she must be!"

"Yes," Roseanna answered innocently. "This weather is so depressing."

"Indeed it is," Evelina agreed.

However, nothing in the world could dampen their enthusiasm for their coming-out ball. They had waited too long and sighed too many impatient sighs to permit anything or anyone to postpone it now.

As they surveyed their finished attire in the mirror in the front hall, their excitement started to mount. Both Roseanna and Evelina wore white crepe gowns, the former with a round neck, the latter with a V neck, over white satin slips.

Their hair was longer than it had been. Roseanna had hers *à la grecque,* with long dark ringlets falling behind her in which were intertwined artificial white flowers. Evelina, on the other hand, preferred a silver tocque to set off her own lustrous curls.

Though Mrs. Poulet had complained bitterly that the dresses this year were too short and afforded too liberal a view of her daughter's and her niece's ankles, the cousins had pleaded with her to let them wear the latest styles. And they had had their way.

"What do you think of us, Mama?" Roseanna asked as her mother joined them shortly before the first guests were due to arrive.

"Yes, Aunt," Evelina said, "tell us your opinion of our gowns. Aren't they divine?"

Mrs. Poulet studied the cousins. Surveying their eager expressions brought back memories of her own first ball. In a split second, her mind had traveled forward to the time she had met her husband.

"Beautiful!" she murmured. "If only your father were alive to see you, Roseanna!"

A shadow crossed Roseanna's face. "Yes, it would be perfect if he were here," she stated.

But Mr. Poulet had died nearly two years ago, after the wedding of their friend Harriet Ashley. And since that time, Mrs. Poulet, a young but grieving widow, had worn deepest mourning. Nothing would induce her to part with her somber wardrobe. Even on this joyful occasion she had donned a black velvet ensemble.

"Aren't you going to wear something more cheerful?" Evelina had questioned when Mrs. Poulet's choice of attire was first mooted.

Mrs. Poulet had bridled. "The death of one's husband is not a laughing matter, miss!" she had declared.

"I'm sure Evelina didn't mean it like that, Mama," Roseanna had soothed.

"No, indeed," Evelina had assured her aunt.

Mrs. Poulet had then archly stated that she had decided on black velvet because, in case no one had noticed, it had been rather cold lately, even for this time of year.

"But surely you will become warm dancing!" Evelina had protested.

"Heavens! *I* shall not dance, Evelina!" Mrs. Poulet had cried. "I would only recall what happiness it was to dance with dear Mr. Poulet when he was alive—and then I should be bound to weep."

"That would never do," Roseanna had said.

"No, indeed, it wouldn't," Evelina had been forced to add.

"But you will try to enjoy yourself, won't you, Mama?" Roseanna said.

"Of course," Mrs. Poulet had responded. "But it won't be easy, you know. In fact, to tell the truth, my dears, it will be impossible. Without my dear husband at my side . . ." She had halted and clasped her hands to her bosom. "Alas! Why was I left alive on this earth without him! What a cruel fate!"

Roseanna and Evelina had exchanged glances. To have made any comment would have led to trouble, so they had chosen to remain silent and the discussion had ended.

Looking at her mother's black gown that night, though, Roseanna could not help wondering whether it was really necessary. Was it her imagination, or was Mrs. Poulet's grief these days a little bit affected?

Roseanna recollected that Evelina had remarked, not so long ago, that it seemed sometimes as if Mrs. Poulet was carrying on her mourning to impress someone. Roseanna had been shocked then, but now she could not help asking herself if Evelina had not been right.

"Naturally I know that Mama and Papa loved each other dearly," Roseanna reflected, "but ...."

Then a knock on the door interrupted her reverie. The first of the guests had arrived and there was no time to stand still and brood.

Hot punch was served, and soon the dancing began. . . .

It was a while before Roseanna was free. When she had a moment, she glanced around at her mother to ascertain how she was bearing up. She spotted Mrs. Poulet seated at the far end of the ballroom, looking apprehensive and ill at ease.

Roseanna sought out her cousin.

"I think something is worrying Mama," she remarked.

Evelina gazed at her aunt. "I believe you are right," she answered.

"Come with me, then, and help me find out what it is," Roseanna exhorted.

"Very well."

The cousins made their way towards Mrs. Poulet.

"Hello, Aunt," Evelina said bluntly. "How are you? Well?"

Mrs. Poulet seemed startled by the question.

"Quite well, thank you," she responded. "Why?"

"We thought you were a trifle pale," Evelina replied. "Didn't we?"

"Yes," Roseanna concurred.

"It is the light," Mrs. Poulet returned. "Merely the light."

"Are you sure?" Roseanna inquired.

"Perfectly," Mrs. Poulet answered.

"There isn't anything the matter, is there?" Roseanna persisted.

"No. No. Nothing," Mrs. Poulet lied. "You two run along now and have a good time."

Roseanna saw through her mother's deception.

"How can we enjoy ourselves when we know there is something troubling you, Mama?" she demanded.

"Pshaw!" Mrs. Poulet exclaimed.

"Come now, Aunt," Evelina remonstrated. "We cannot be happy unless you are too. What is it? Tell us."

Mrs. Poulet sighed. "It is nothing, really," she insisted. "A trifle; a bagatelle—nothing more."

"What is it, then?" Roseanna queried.

"Are you sure you want to know?"

"Yes, of course, Mama."

Mrs. Poulet made a despairing gesture.

"I did not want to alarm you, but Denis has not yet arrived," she observed.

Roseanna, who had covertly included Count Czarski's name on the invitation to her cousin, froze. Everyone else had come, so what was keeping them? She thought suddenly of the château in Craonne where Denis Martin had been a prisoner. What if something had gone wrong? What if they had both been captured and killed? What if she never saw Count Czarski—or her cousin—again?

Her face clouded. "I noticed," she said.

Mrs. Poulet concealed her smile. She knew nothing about Roseanna's meeting with the count. She presumed that her daughter's concern was entirely for her cousin.

"But why should that alarm us?" Evelina wanted to

know. "Denis might be delayed by this dreadful snow, mightn't he?"

Mrs. Poulet gave her a pitying look. "The last news I had of him, through my dearest brother, was that he was in France," she pointed out. "A prisoner."

Roseanna gave a tiny scream of anguish. "A prisoner?" she repeated, for all the world as if she had had no idea. "Oh, no!"

"How terrible!" Evelina exclaimed, also feigning ignorance. "No wonder you have been upset, Aunt!"

"Yes. Exactly. I—" Mrs. Poulet began.

She was about to proceed, when the door of the ballroom opened and Denis Martin appeared. The three women uttered cries of delight at seeing him. They were on their feet in an instant and embraced him warmly.

Only when she had greeted her cousin as she was expected to did Roseanna allow herself to look and see whether he had brought the count with him. To her relief, he had, and he proceeded to introduce him.

Roseanna congratulated herself that she played her part well. She, who was untutored in the art of dissembling, managed to pretend that she had never before met the count. And neither gentleman let on that Roseanna had invited Count Czarski. Roseanna smiled to herself. Even Evelina didn't know about that.

"I hope you don't mind my bringing Marek," Denis apologized to his aunt.

Mrs. Poulet was deliriously happy to see her nephew safe and sound. She was prepared to overlook everything else.

"Of course not," she replied. "Your friends are welcome here."

Denis Martin smiled. So accommodating was Mrs. Poulet that she had even acquiesced to the four of them being on first-name terms.

"You must partner Roseanna, Denis!" Mrs. Poulet insisted rapturously. "Let me see you together, my dears, and I shall be happy!"

Denis turned to Roseanna and asked her dutifully

if she had a dance for him. Roseanna, equally dutifully, answered that he could have the next one.

As soon as this was settled, Count Czarski spoke.

"Mrs. Poulet," he said, "I hope I do not presume, but may I have this dance?"

Mrs. Poulet appeared flattered by his attentions. For a moment both Roseanna and Evelina thought that the count's charm had pierced her armor.

"I would love to, Lord Czarski," she returned, "but I regret I must decline. I am still in mourning for my husband."

"I understand, madam," Count Czarski assured her.

"Perhaps Evelina will oblige you," Mrs. Poulet suggested.

"Miss Poulet?" Count Czarski questioned.

Evelina curtsied and accepted.

Even when they were not dancing together, Roseanna felt the count's eyes on her. She was hardly out of his sight, and the moment she was free he was at her side.

"Tell me what happened after you brought us home," Roseanna asked as they whirled around the floor.

Count Czarski gave a tiny shrug. "Nothing much," he answered, speaking lightly. "I was fortunate that the fog lifted when it did, since that made it easier to travel."

"Did you go to France?"

"Yes."

"What happened when you arrived?"

Again that little noncommittal shrug. "It wasn't exciting, if that is what you were thinking," he stated.

"No. I ... I was afraid for you." She shivered involuntarily. "I thought it would be dangerous."

Count Czarski's expression altered slightly, in a way she did not understand.

"It would have been dangerous if anyone who knew that I was supposed to be in England had recognized me," he conceded. "But, as it was, everything went smoothly. Denis and I were able to leave France in a matter of days."

As Roseanna listened to him, she wondered how much he was minimizing the perils. What narrow escapes had they had? How difficult had it really been?

She longed to question him further, but her instincts warned her not to.

As they waltzed together later that evening, they talked of generalities, and Roseanna found herself reflecting on what a curious mixture of reticence and frankness Count Czarski was. She was glad they were on first-name terms. It was easier for her to call him *Marek* than *Count Czarski*.

"He can be so . . . so open, and yet," she thought, "so mysterious."

She had the vague feeling that Count Czarski led a double life, that he showed people only what he wanted them to see.

"No. No. You're imagining it," she told herself silently.

Roseanna and Evelina both had a dance free, and they decided to sit together on the edge of the ballroom.

"What do you think of it so far?" Roseanna questioned.

"Our coming-out ball?" Evelina countered.

"Yes."

"I'm enjoying it immensely!" Evelina exclaimed. "I wish it could last the entire week!"

"Me too!" Roseanna agreed. Then she gave a gasp of astonishment. "Good gracious! Look!"

Evelina turned her head in time to see Mrs. Poulet standing up for the next cotillion.

"Well!" Evelina declared.

After her aunt had protested so vigorously that she would not dance!

"And with Mr. Sandford, too!" Roseanna cried.

Evelina regarded Mr. Sandford with a mixture of awe and disapproval.

"Mind you, he has been very attentive to Aunt ever since your father's funeral," she said.

"Yes, he has," Roseanna mused.

She recalled that he had worked for the same firm

23

as her father and that he had come to represent a branch of it at the funeral.

"Do you think he is a decent sort of man?" she wondered.

"I'm sure he is," Evelina responded. "But he's a bit young for Aunt, isn't he?"

"I don't know. How old is he?"

"Thirty. Slightly less, I believe."

"A little young, perhaps," Roseanna replied. She bit her lip. "I don't really like him. Do you?"

"No, I don't. But I can't say why ... unless it is because he is a bit of a stuffed shirt."

"Hmmmm, yes," Roseanna murmured uneasily. "You know, in many ways, Mr. Sandford is older than Mama."

"You're right. He is so inflexible in his outlook. His attitudes are already quite set—just like an old man's."

Roseanna nodded in assent. "He's not a bad chap, but ..." She sighed forlornly. "I do hope Mama takes a dislike to him. I would hate to have him for my stepfather!"

Evelina laughed. "There is no need to worry about that!" she returned.

"Isn't there?" Roseanna asked plaintively. "Don't you believe Mama will marry again?"

"Not until she has seen you safely disposed of," Evelina answered. "*You* needn't fret."

"Well, that's a comfort," Roseanna stated. "I suppose she will wait until we are both settled before she remarries—if she does."

"I suppose so."

"You don't sound positive."

"Well, she might wait until you are off her hands, but what about me?"

"She'll want to see you married too. Won't she?"

Evelina considered the question. Society frowned on widows remarrying. It seemed somehow disloyal to one's dear departed. Of course there was nothing to prevent them, but they must have the decency to wait until *all* the eligible young, unattached female members of the family were wed.

"Yes," Evelina decided. "She'll see us both married

24

before she takes the plunge again. What's the matter now?"

"Nothing. It's just that I . . . I don't want her to keep on seeing Mr. Sandford," Roseanna said hesitantly. "He . . . He isn't good enough for her."

"No, Grandmama dear," Evelina teased, at this remark, which was more typical of an elderly lady than someone their age.

Roseanna giggled. "You are terrible!" she exclaimed. "But I really do not think he is suitable. Do you?"

"No. Let us keep our fingers crossed that Aunt agrees with us."

"Oh, this cold!" Mrs. Poulet exclaimed at breakfast the next morning. "It really is getting to me!"

"Me too," Roseanna said.

"And me," Evelina echoed.

Mrs. Poulet grimaced. They had been driven to eating in the kitchen, since that was the first room in the house to warm up. Imagine! The lady of the house compelled to dine in the kitchen!

"Do you know what the latest is?" Mrs. Poulet asked. And then, without waiting for an answer, she announced: "The Thames is frozen solid."

"What!" Roseanna gasped.

"But it can't be!" Evelina exclaimed.

Such a thing had not happened since the reign of Charles II!

"Well, it is," Mrs. Poulet reiterated. "From Blackfriars' Bridge to London Bridge. Of course the *Times* says that it isn't safe, but even they admit that it is frozen."

"Well!" Evelina declared. "Who would have thought it!"

"Who indeed!" Roseanna cried.

"No wonder we felt so cold when we got to bed last night!"

"Mmmmm. No wonder. Is there any more toast, Mama?"

"Not unless you make it," her mother responded.

"Yes, I shall," Roseanna said, taking the toasting

25

fork and creeping as close to the blazing fire as she dared.

Neither she nor Evelina thought more about the frozen waterway until the following day, when they discovered that someone had taken a sheep out onto the ice and roasted it over a coal fire. Then they had sold slices of it at a shilling a piece as "Lapland mutton."

"Sounds exciting," Evelina commented.

"Does rather," Roseanna concurred.

Their imaginations were further fired when they learned that a Frost Fair had been initiated on the Thames.

"Please, please, please, can we go?" Roseanna besought her mother.

"No," Mrs. Poulet replied.

"Why not?" Roseanna wanted to know.

"It is too far away from here," Mrs. Poulet informed her.

"It isn't really," Evelina contradicted. "It wouldn't take us half an hour to get there."

"I think, miss," Mrs. Poulet returned tartly, "it would take a great deal longer than that!"

"Oh, please, Mama," Roseanna begged. "It is the event of a lifetime. Think! The last time the Thames froze over was more than a hundred and fifty years ago!"

"And judging by that," Evelina said, "it will never freeze again as long as we live."

"We'll regret it all our lives if we don't at least see it," Roseanna pleaded. "Oh, do let us go, Mama!"

"Yes, please let us go, Aunt," Evelina added.

"We'll be careful, really we will."

"We won't do anything silly."

Despite their assurances, Mrs. Poulet was reluctant to allow the cousins to wander so far from home. She recalled how, last year, they had narrowly escaped being burned to death when their carriage had caught fire in the Strand, during the illuminations.

But Roseanna and Evelina pointed out that firecrackers had been thrown at the carriage and that this would not happen today. They reminded her that they had been unharmed and accused her of exaggerating the danger.

Eventually Mrs. Poulet saw that she was beaten. After issuing a thousand instructions as to what precautions they should take and what they might do and what they might not do, she permitted them to travel to Blackfriars' Bridge to see the Frost Fair.

Roseanna and Evelina could hardly contain their excitement. They could see the booths and the people milling about on the ice from the bridge, where their carriage deposited them.

"Oh, look!" Evelina cried. "Isn't it fantastic!"

"Marvelous!" Roseanna agreed.

"Hurry up and get your skates on!" Evelina exhorted.

Roseanna needed no second admonition.

As soon as they were ready, the cousins hobbled down onto the frozen river. The moment their feet touched the ice, they glided in amongst the crowd.

The Frost Fair had everything. There were swings and bookstalls. One could go dancing on a barge. Booths selling tea, coffee, alcohol, hot pies—indeed, divers refreshments—vied for their attention. Skittles, knock-'em-down games, gambling, and other attractions were offered by enterprising shopkeepers.

"How expensive everything is!" Evelina commented as they went around looking at the curiosities.

"It's all a question of supply and demand," Roseanna replied, mimicking the standard cockney answer to that remark.

And of course the traders who had risked their livelihoods to come out onto the Thames, not knowing how long the fair was going to last, were bound to charge as much as the traffic would bear. What price a once-in-150-years event?

There was no shortage of customers. Everyone who had the time and the money to spare found their way here. Ladies and gentlemen from the West End of London who had never seen a frozen pond, let alone an ice-

27

covered river, shrieked with delight as they slipped and slid this way and that. Working men and women left their offices and factories to catch a glimpse of the Frost Fair. Children screamed with joy at the new sensation of skating.

"It certainly is an experience," Roseanna stated as she and Evelina came to a halt in the middle of the now-solid waterway.

"Yes, it is," Evelina agreed. She gazed around her, and queried suddenly:

"Isn't that Denis over there?"

Roseanna turned in the direction indicated. "Yes, it is," she confirmed. "And there is Marek with him!"

3

"I wonder what brings *them* here," Evelina mused.

"Let's go and ask them," Roseanna urged.

The cousins glided over to where the two men were standing, near the entrance to the fair.

Evelina arrived first.

"Fancy meeting you here," she said as she came to a stop, grinding up the ice with her blades in order to brake.

"Yes, what a coincidence!" Roseanna concurred as she halted. "Isn't it strange that you should come here when we were here!"

"Not really," Denis Martin responded.

"What do you mean?" Evelina demanded.

"I received a frantic note from Aunt," Denis explained. "She wrote that she had allowed the pair of you to go to the Frost Fair, but now she was frightened that something would happen to you."

"Oh, no!" Evelina groaned. "I fear the worst, Roseanna!"

Roseanna swallowed. "You're not supposed to bring us home, are you?" she asked anxiously.

"No," Count Czarski reassured her, "merely to look after you so that you will be all right."

"When *will* Aunt learn that we can take care of ourselves!" Evelina wanted to know.

Roseanna sighed. "We're sorry you had to go to such trouble on our account," she apologized.

"Don't be," Count Czarski said. "We wanted to come."

"Yes," Denis seconded, "to see the fair. What's it like?"

"Unbelievable!" Evelina declared. "You must see the knock-'em-down games, Denis. Do come!"

Before he could protest, she had seized his hand and dragged him across the frozen river.

Count Czarski turned to Roseanna.

"Shall we follow them?" he inquired, offering her his arm.

Roseanna nodded in assent and slipped her hand over his.

"How well he skates!" she thought.

He seemed as at ease on the ice as he had been on the ballroom floor. He could not have been more unconcerned if he had been escorting her into the dining room at North Row.

"But why does he keep looking at me?" Roseanna wondered.

It was not because she was unsteady on her feet. She glanced shyly up at him. And immediately lowered her eyes.

Admiration was something Roseanna was unused to. She did not know how appealing she was in her brown velvet military-style pelisse with its gold-braid trimming. She had no idea how enchanting her matching chocolate-colored turban was. And Count Czarski's gaze—unexpected, and, she was sure, forbidden—confused her.

"Where's Denis?" she questioned abruptly.

Count Czarski came to a standstill.

"I don't know," he answered.

"Can't you see him?"

"No."

"What about Evelina?"

"No."

"Oh, dear. We've lost them!"

"Don't fret," Count Czarski advised. "They'll soon realize that we are not with them any more. Then they'll retrace their steps and come after us."

"I suppose so," Roseanna said uncertainly.

"I am sure this is not proper," she reflected silently.

Here she was, scarcely "out" a week and on the ice alone with a strange man. What ever would her mother say?

"Let's go and see one of the printing presses," Count Czarski suggested.

"Very well," Roseanna replied.

They made their way through the crowd toward a section of the Frost Fair where various printing presses had been set up and were producing a selection of pamphlets. Roseanna watched, fascinated, as the type was set and the presses made to work before her very eyes. She read with amusement the treatises on the frost, on the Thames, and on the fair itself.

"Would you like one?" Count Czarski asked.

Roseanna glanced sharply at him.

"Er—um—hmmmm," she stammered, uncertain as to what he meant.

Did he intend to give her one? Words of warning and of disapproval about young ladies receiving gifts from men rang in her ears. She could hear the lecture her mother would give her if she accepted anything from him.

Count Czarski seemed to sense the reason for her hesitation.

"I know I would," he remarked, "but there are so many to choose from. They are so prolific. Rather like the leaves in autumn, don't you think?"

"I . . . I don't understand," Roseanna responded.

"Have you never saved an autumn leaf to remind you of a pleasant summer?"

Roseanna started. "I . . ." How on earth had he known that? "Yes. I have," she admitted.

"Can't you see the similarity?"

Suddenly she did. The broadsides were as profuse and plentiful as falling leaves—they were just as small, just as fragile, and just as innocent.

"Yes. You are right," Roseanna mused.

She had not regarded it like that before, but now that he mentioned it, it was an excellent simile. If a man gave a woman a leaf, she could hardly call it a present, could she? Thus, if a man gave a woman a sheet of printed paper at a fair, the same applied. There would be no need to feel guilty . . . or to tell Mama!

Count Czarski smiled as he saw her face clear.

"Let me buy you one," he offered.

"Which one?" Roseanna questioned.

He indicated a stall Roseanna had not previously noticed. It was selling tracts that she had not seen earlier, discoursing on "Freedom of the Press."

Who could take offense at a souvenir that was so instructive?

"That would be nice," she replied.

Count Czarski purchased one for her.

Roseanna was more delighted with his gift than she could say. "Thank you," she murmured as he placed the paper into her hand.

She was unaware, as she cast her eyes down and the color suffused her cheek, how attractive she looked. She did not know how expressive her face was and how much joy she revealed.

"The pleasure was mine," Count Czarski returned.

Two seconds later, Denis Martin and Evelina skated up to them. There was no word about getting lost. Evelina, at any rate, seemed quite unconcerned about that.

"So there you are!" she exclaimed. "See what Denis has given me!"

Obediently, Roseanna and Count Czarski looked. In Evelina's hand was a pamphlet similar to the one the count had bought for Roseanna. It was one of many sold as "proof" for future generations that one had walked on the frozen Thames.

"How nice!" Roseanna declared.

Then Evelina observed the paper in her cousin's hand.

"What have you got there?" she inquired.

Roseanna showed her Count Czarski's little present. Evelina perused it and passed it across to Denis Martin, who smiled as he read the words.

"If anyone had asked me which you would buy, Marek," he said, "I would have bet a pony it would be that one."

A "pony" was slang for twenty-five pounds, quite a lot of money.

Count Czarski smiled enigmatically. "You know me well, Denis," he commented.

Denis Martin clapped his friend on the back. "You're right there. I think I can safely say I know you better than anyone!" he cried. And then, before Count Czarski could respond: "Are any of you hungry? I know I am. Shall we dine here? Or ...?"

"What a wonderful idea!" Evelina enthused. "I confess I'm famished!"

"Yes," Roseanna added, "I am hungry too."

"It's the cold air," Count Czarski stated. "It gives one an appetite."

"Yes, it does," Denis agreed. "Now, which booth shall we favor with our custom for lunch?"

"Let's skate round and see which looks the best," Count Czarski suggested.

"Good idea," Denis replied.

"Come," Count Czarski commanded.

He linked his arm with Roseanna's once more and began to glide over the smooth surface of the ice, with Denis and Evelina following.

Roseanna wondered if her cousins would notice the familiarity of his actions, but they did not remark on it.

Eventually, they selected a booth in the middle of the ice which served decent hot food. Although it was not the sort of formal meal they were accustomed to, they enjoyed it.

"That was delicious," Evelina said when they finished. "But I do wish it were warmer!"

"Me too," Roseanna concurred. "It is very cold here."

"Indeed it is!" Evelina declared. "My toes are numb and my fingers quite stiff!"

33

"Mine too," Roseanna murmured.

"We can't have that," Count Czarski returned. "Isn't there somewhere we can go to warm up, Denis?"

"Let me think," Denis Martin answered. "I know. The George Inn in Southwark."

That was the best place. It was close at hand and it was respectable. Without further ado, the four of them made their way to the south side of the Thames, removed their skates, and walked the short distance from the snowbound Pepper Alley Steps to the Borough High Street, off which the George Inn was situated.

Used as she was to seeing galleried inns, Roseanna could not but admire the George, with its wooden balconies rising tier after tier, seeming to stretch to the heavens themselves. And how good it was to be warm once more! To sit by the fire sipping mulled ale, to feel one's frozen toes thaw out, to scoff thickly buttered crumpets and savor the cozy intimacy of the hearth.

"Now that we're warm once more," Evelina stated, "let's go back to the Frost Fair."

"Yes, let's," Roseanna seconded. "We haven't seen everything yet. Please, let's go back."

"I'm game," Denis said. "Are you, Marek?"

"Who could refuse two such enchanting petitioners?" Count Czarski countered gallantly.

But, though he included Evelina in his speech, his eyes were all the while on Roseanna.

Roseanna felt as if she were a bubbling saucepan about to boil over. She could hardly wait to get her skates on. But her eagerness made her clumsy. She fumbled, and the others were ready before her.

Evelina and Denis were on the ice first. They moved away from the edge towards the crowded stalls. Count Czarski followed them.

At last Roseanna stepped onto the frozen surface. Flushed with excitement, she spun round and round on the same spot, like a top. By the time she stopped twirling in a circle, she was very giddy. She swayed and slithered about in an attempt to keep her balance.

Dizzy as Roseanna was, she was not aware that she

was going backwards, away from the safe, solid area. She did not realize that she had gone too far until she halted to catch her breath. Then there was a resounding crack as the piece of ice on which she had been standing parted from the main body.

Roseanna screamed in terror as her predicament became clear to her.

Denis and Evelina heard her. They gasped in horror as they saw what was happening, and started to skate toward her. But they had been a great distance away from Roseanna when she cried out, and even as they raced across the ice, the swirling waters of the Thames began to take her away from them.

After her initial fright, Roseanna was shocked into immobility. She was so terrified that she could do nothing except stand erect and stare as the gap between the ice floe where she was and the Frost Fair grew wider and wider.

4

Suddenly Roseanna was aware of Count Czarski. With a mighty bound he leaped gracefully onto the ice beside her.

"Get down!" he ordered.

Roseanna was galvanized into action. She did as he commanded and laid herself flat on the ice.

It was only just in time. The swift-moving current was taking them toward the arches of London Bridge. This was the most treacherous part of the entire Thames. The eddies and whirlpools created here were so dangerous that even skilled oarsmen took their lives into their hands when they shot through.

Count Czarski had his arm around Roseanna. He shielded her with his body. She did not know how glad he was that she had moved the moment he gave the word. Standing upright as she had been, not looking where she was going, she could so easily have been knocked on the head by one of the stone pillars of London Bridge. If that had happened, she would undoubtedly have fallen into the water and then nothing could have saved her!

Roseanna shivered with fear and cold. All around her she could see the menacing waves with their freezing wet fingers trying to seize her and drag her under. As the frozen raft entered the dark damp hell beneath London Bridge, the sound of the water splashing reverberated evilly and Roseanna trembled.

"Don't be alarmed," Count Czarski said gently. "We'll make it."

As he finished speaking, they emerged from the blackness and found themselves being drawn toward the shore at Billingsgate. There they were seen by the Thames boatmen, who soon came out to rescue them.

Roseanna heaved a sigh of relief as the count handed her from the ice into one of the ferry boats. Then she fainted.

When Roseanna came to, she was in a public house. The count and Denis were with her. So was Evelina, who was anxiously trying to coax her cousin to drink some brandy. Roseanna swallowed the liquid, which burned like fire as it went down her throat.

"You gave us a terrific fright!" Evelina declared.

"I'm sorry," Roseanna murmured.

As she spoke, a hand touched hers. A light caress. So swift that no one could have seen it. No one but herself would even be aware of it.

Roseanna knew it was the count who had touched her, and she felt immediately better. Strange how reassuring such a little gesture could be!

"You won't tell Mama, will you?" Roseanna questioned.

"Not likely!" Evelina cried.

"We'd never hear the end of it!" Denis exclaimed.

"Yes, indeed," Count Czarski concurred. "After all, we were sent here to make sure that sort of thing did not occur."

"Exactly," Denis agreed. "We won't breathe a word of it, we promise."

"Heavens, what an idea!" Evelina gasped. "It was

37

difficult enough to get Aunt to allow us out after what happened during the illuminations. If news of this reaches her, we'll never be permitted to go anywhere on our own again!"

Roseanna tried to smile.

"Are you feeling better?" Count Czarski asked.

"Yes, thank you," she managed to answer.

"Well, in that case," Denis responded, "shall we leave here?"

Roseanna nodded in assent. She was helped to her feet by Evelina, and the four of them took a hackney carriage and traveled in the direction of the Frost Fair once more.

"You're not the only one to be carried away by the ice," Denis remarked.

"Oh?" Roseanna queried.

"There was an old man and a boy who were swept down the river earlier today," Denis informed her. "But they were rescued before they came to any harm."

"Oh," Roseanna murmured.

"I think the newspapers will print that story rather than this one," Count Czarski commented. "Your press is so gallant, though. Even if they do make mention of our accident, they would not be so cruel as to give the names of the ladies involved."

Roseanna considered his statement.

"That's true," she responded. "Where are we going?"

"Back to the Frost Fair," Denis replied promptly.

"Oh, no!" Roseanna protested.

"But I thought you enjoyed it," Denis returned.

"Yes I did...very much...but..." Roseanna answered. "I...I'm tired. I would rather go home."

"Not right now, surely!" Evelina exclaimed. "You are deathly pale. If we are going to prevent Aunt from finding out about this unfortunate incident, then you need some color in your cheeks."

"Definitely," Count Czarski concurred.

"Oh, dear," Roseanna stated. "Where can we go?"

"What about coming to the Albany for tea?" Denis suggested.

"A splendid idea!" Evelina declared.

"Yes," Roseanna agreed. "Thank you."

38

"Not at all," Denis added.

He instructed the hackney-carriage driver to take them to the Albany, where the four of them had tea in the sitting room.

Roseanna was increasingly aware of the count's presence. It wasn't anything she could put her finger on, except . . . he seemed to be watching her the entire time. When they had first met, she had found this habit of his unnerving. Now, however, she was beginning to enjoy his attentions.

"Do the others know?" Roseanna wondered.

She glanced apprehensively at them. But they had not noticed how much Count Czarski was paying his addresses to her. How could they? His manner was so easy and relaxed. He conversed freely with Denis, and with Evelina as much as with her. He did not appear to monopolize her, as she had seen other men do when they were in company with women.

"Maybe I am imagining it," Roseanna thought.

But the moment the idea had crossed her mind, she dismissed it. Count Czarski was interested in her. It might not be obvious to the others, but it was to her.

Mrs. Poulet was waiting for Roseanna and Evelina when they went back to North Row.

"You have been gone a long time!" she exclaimed.

"Yes, Mama," Roseanna agreed.

"Did you enjoy yourselves?" Mrs. Poulet wanted to know.

"Yes, Aunt, very much," Evelina answered.

"You didn't catch cold, did you?" Mrs. Poulet questioned.

"No, Mama."

"No, indeed, Aunt."

"Well, come into the drawing room and tell me everything that happened," Mrs. Poulet ordered. "I am dying to hear what you two have been doing."

Once in the warmth of the drawing room, Roseanna and Evelina plunged in, excitedly describing the Frost

Fair and how they met Denis Martin and Count Czarski. They told Mrs. Poulet about the lunch at the George Inn and that they had returned to the Frost Fair afterwards...

"...but we didn't stay long," Evelina said.

"Why not?" Mrs. Poulet wondered.

"Too cold," Evelina replied promptly.

"Yes. It made us numb," Roseanna clarified. "I couldn't feel my toes, and my fingers hurt, so we decided to leave."

"Very wise," Mrs. Poulet commented. "Did you go anywhere else?"

"Yes," Roseanna answered. "Denis invited us to the Albany for tea."

Mrs. Poulet seemed very pleased about that.

"How nice of him!" she declared. "How sensible to take you there to warm up before you came home. Don't you think that was kind of him?"

"Yes, Aunt."

"Yes, Mama."

Mrs. Poulet, however, was not satisfied with their response. She continued to commend her nephew for his good sense for several minutes before she permitted them to proceed to another topic.

The long-awaited thaw commenced that weekend. The snow melted, the Frost Fair dissolved into nothing, the mail coaches started to arrive on time once more, and life began to return to normal in the capital.

During the next few weeks Roseanna and Evelina had dozens of engagements to fulfill. Their coming-out ball had produced a flood of invitations: balls, dinners, trips to the theater, concerts, and soirees. They lost count of the number of pairs of dancing slippers they wore through and the gloves they mislaid.

They saw little of either Denis Martin or Count Czarski. When they did meet, it was usually at a crowded reception or some occasion where there was not really any chance to talk.

"...and I never see Marek if any of the royal family is present," Roseanna mused silently.

Why not? Didn't he wish to be noticed? For her own part, she had not met a man or a woman who wouldn't give their eye teeth to be singled out at a reception by the Prince Regent or one of the other royal dukes. Surely Count Czarski was no different? He wanted society's approbation too, didn't he?

Roseanna frowned. "Denis never misses a party where the Prince Regent is a guest," she reflected. "But Marek..."

Count Czarski seemed to be deliberately avoiding crossing His Royal Highness's path.

"But why?" Roseanna wondered. There was no reason, unless... "Perhaps it is because he has not yet been presented."

If that were the case, it could pose problems as far as etiquette was concerned. It might be awkward for everyone involved. Yes, that was definitely the logical explanation. All the same...

"Roseanna! Are you ready?"

Evelina's impatient question broke into her cousin's reverie.

"Yes," Roseanna responded. "Coming."

The Prince Regent was going to be at the dinner they had been invited to that night. They must not be late.

Denis Martin, in his official capacity, proposed the next toast:

"To peace."

It occurred to Roseanna, as she joined in with the others in echoing the sentiment, that it did not seem as unrealistic to wish for peace now as it had when she was a child.

Every day the papers printed news of the French forces retreating. They seemed to have lost their strength after that disastrous attack on Moscow, and their progress across Europe had become a series of defeats. The Allied armies, on the other hand, had won victory upon victory as they advanced closer and closer to Paris.

"I suppose it is only a matter of time before peace

is declared," Roseanna reflected. "But what will happen to France then?"

The newspapers had no doubt that the Bourbons would be restored to their throne. At least once a week one of them carried a report on the character of one or other member of the Bourbon royal house: the Duc de Berry; the Duc d'Angoulême; King Louis XVIII; the Comte d'Artois...

"If they go on much longer, I shall be familiar with every single member of the French royal family," Roseanna mused silently.

As the dinner drew to a close, their host announced that the Prince Regent would be able to stay for the first five dances only. Then, regretfully, he had to take his leave of the company.

To Roseanna's delight, she was one of the lucky ladies chosen to be His Royal Highness's partner.

Later, when the Prince Regent had gone, Roseanna, in a state of rare excitement, located Evelina.

"Guess what!" she exclaimed breathlessly.

"What?" Evelina asked her.

"The Grand Duchess of Oldenburg is coming to London tomorrow."

"Who's she?"

Roseanna raised her eyes to the heavens.

"Oh, you!" she cried. "*Everyone* has heard of the Grand Duchess of Oldenburg!"

"I am *not* everyone," Evelina retorted.

"Hrmph!"

"Well? Who is she?"

"The Czar's sister," Roseanna clarified. "She is on a state visit to England."

"Oh, yes?" Evelina queried. "Who told you that?"

"His Royal Highness the Prince Regent! We danced a quadrille together!"

"I know. I saw you. Congratulations."

"Thank you."

"Did he talk to you, then?"

"Yes, he did."

"About the Grand Duchess?"

"Precisely. He said what a refreshing change it was to speak to someone sensible like me."

"Ye-e-es. Hmmmm."

Roseanna gave an exasperated snort. "I am not even going to ask what *that* means," she told her cousin. "His Royal Highness intimated that it was extremely important because the Grand Duchess of Oldenburg is His Imperial Majesty's favorite sister and it is a sign of great trust on the Czar's part to send Her Imperial Highness here."

"Oh, I see."

"You don't sound particularly enthusiastic."

"I simply don't understand what all the fuss is about."

Roseanna grimaced. "She is at Sheerness today," she started. "Tomorrow she will drive through London. The Duke of Clarence will be with her and—"

"A parade, you mean?" Evelina interrupted eagerly.

"Exactly."

"How wonderful! Why didn't you say so in the first place? Let's go and see her!"

"Yes, let's," Roseanna agreed enthusiastically. And then her face fell.

"What is it?"

"Permission. Mama told me before we left that she had a headache. And you know her headaches. They last for days."

Evelina bit her lip. That was, unfortunately, perfectly true. If Mrs. Poulet had one of her migraines, she would take to her bed at the earliest opportunity, and that meant that Roseanna and Evelina, since they had no one to chaperone them, would be confined to the house—unless of course it was something like tonight, where the Prince Regent was expected.

"... And you know what Mama is about the two of us being in a crowd on our own," Roseanna added, breaking into her cousin's reverie.

"Don't remind me!" Evelina exhorted grimly. "You don't suppose we could sneak out and ..."

Roseanna shook her head in negation. "If we ever did that, Mama would be sure to find out about it," she pointed out. "And then she would get us a duenna who would be so strict that our lives would be intolerable."

"How ghastly! So tomorrow is out, then, is it?"

43

Roseanna considered for a moment. "Not necessarily," she replied.

"What do you mean?"

"Denis is here. We can ask him if he will escort us. Mama won't turn us down then."

"Horrors!"

"What? But—"

"You're right, but I saw Denis leaving only a moment ago."

"Quick! We must catch him!"

The two of them raced toward the magnificent entrance of the house. There, on the steps, about to enter his carriage, was Denis Martin. And with him, having come to collect him, was Count Czarski.

"Oh, Denis!" Roseanna exclaimed. "Thank heavens we've caught you!"

Denis Martin stared at her in surprise. "Why?" he inquired. "What's the matter?"

Excitedly the cousins told him their predicament. Denis Martin listened thoughtfully, as did Count Czarski.

"We should be happy to accompany you ladies," Count Czarski remarked. "Wouldn't we, Denis?"

"Yes. Delighted," Denis Martin concurred. "I'll talk to Aunt now, shall I? Put it to her as if it were my idea all along?"

"Yes, please," Roseanna responded.

"Oh, thank you!" Evelina cried.

The crowds became dense very quickly and Roseanna and Evelina were glad that they had arrived early, even though it meant standing in the biting wind for several minutes. As they were at the front, on the edge of the pavement, with Count Czarski and Denis Martin directly behind them to prevent them from being jostled, they knew that they would have an excellent view to compensate them for any unpleasantness they might endure.

While the four of them were waiting, the Grand Duchess of Oldenburg had entered London via Westminster Bridge. Her route took her along Parliament

Street into Horse Guards' Parade. From there her carriage went through the Stable Yard of St. James's Palace into St. James's Street towards the Pulteney Grand Hotel, where Her Imperial Highness was to stay.

The first intimation Roseanna and Evelina had that the royal party was approaching was the sound of horses' hooves in the distance and loud cheering from the crowd in the Stable Yard.

Presently two light horsemen came into view and Roseanna found herself cheering as she caught sight of the Duke of Clarence's traveling chariot and four, with His Grace the Duke of Clarence inside as well as an officer whom she did not know.

Two more light horsemen, two footmen, and an outrider in royal livery followed. Then the royal carriage itself, drawn by four bays, belonging to the Prince Regent, swept majestically by.

"Will you just look at that dreadful hat!" Evelina exclaimed as it passed her.

Like her cousin, Roseanna was riveted by it. Its wearer was Her Imperial Highness the Grand Duchess of Oldenburg. But that fact did not signify. The hat was hideous—absolutely frightful!

"It reminds me of a coal scuttle!" Roseanna breathed.

"Doesn't it, though!" Evelina concurred.

"Do you think it will catch on?"

"Undoubtedly. Whatever I think is perfectly revolting usually does."

Roseanna laughed. "Poor Evelina!" she commiserated. "But it is an unfortunate hat. Why, one cannot see anything of her face!"

"Maybe she is so appallingly plain that she is afraid to reveal it," Evelina suggested.

"Or so ravishingly beautiful that she does not wish to," Roseanna murmured.

There was scarcely a moment to glance at the other women traveling in the royal carriage with the grand duchess. Roseanna and Evelina recognized Princess Lieven, the wife of the Russian Ambassador, whom they had seen before. Now, there was an ugly woman. Why, her nose was indecently long!

But the other two ladies in the vehicle neither Roseanna nor Evelina knew by sight. They reckoned that they must be Russian courtiers—princesses probably. Someone had mentioned that they had a plethora of princesses over there.

Roseanna turned to the count, who was standing behind her.

"What do you think of it so far?" she asked.

As she finished speaking she caught a glimpse of his face. There was an expression of such terrible animosity on it that it sent a shiver down her spine.

5

Almost immediately, Count Czarski's face softened.

"Most agreeable," he answered. "I like your Duke of Clarence. He is a pleasant-looking man."

"Yes," Roseanna concurred.

Her heart was thumping wildly. Why should he regard the Russian royal family in that manner? It had been at them his murderous enmity had been directed, hadn't it? Or had he been thinking of something—perhaps someone—different?

Roseanna trembled as the procession continued with a carriage occupied by Prince Gargarine and General Turner. Then came the Russian ambassador, accompanied solely by his countrymen.

"If it is the Russians..." Roseanna thought.

She stole a glance at the count. The hate-filled gaze was back. It lasted barely a second, but the intensity of it! That was what frightened Roseanna.

"What can I say?" Roseanna wondered. "Nothing. He will deny it. Or... he will be angry with me..."

Presently a body of light horsemen brought the parade to an end.

"That was most enjoyable," Evelina stated.

"Yes," Roseanna added. "Thank you for bringing us."

"The pleasure was ours," Count Czarski responded.

Roseanna and Evelina arrived home as Mrs. Poulet and Mr. Sandford were finishing their tea.

"There is some in the pot if you would like a cup," Mrs. Poulet informed them.

"Thank you, Mama," Roseanna replied.

"Yes, thank you, Aunt," Evelina said. "We could do with a nice hot drink."

They seated themselves at the tea table opposite Mrs. Poulet and waited while the tea was poured. It was with something of a shock that they suddenly realized that Mrs. Poulet was no longer wearing her customary completely black attire.

Roseanna and Evelina exchanged stunned glances.

Evelina recovered first. "That gown becomes you, Aunt," she commented.

Mrs. Poulet preened. "You think so?" she queried.

"Yes, indeed," Evelina answered. "The *color* does something for you."

"Thank you," Mrs. Poulet returned, less enthusiastically.

She understood the implied criticism in the slight emphasis Evelina had laid on the word *color*. She knew that it was her niece's way of reminding her how she had refused to put on anything but black even for their coming-out party. Yet here she was today, scarcely two months later, in a white dress with black trimming—half mourning, no less!

It was Mr. Sandford's influence. That was as plain as a pikestaff. He had already made his presence felt when he got her to dance at their coming-out ball. Now he had persuaded her to come out of her full mourning.

And what next? That was what was troubling the cousins.

"I hear you saw the Grand Duchess of Oldenburg's entry into London," Mr. Sandford stated.

"Yes, we did," Evelina replied. "It was very interesting."

"Tell us about it," Mrs. Poulet exhorted.

Roseanna and Evelina recounted how Denis Martin and Count Czarski had taken them to St. James's Street. They explained how they had had a place where they could see well without being jostled by the crowd. They described the parade in detail, especially the Grand Duchess's hat, which had totally hidden her countenance from view.

"We enjoyed it very much," Evelina observed. "The only thing is, it didn't last long, which was a pity."

"Yes," Roseanna agreed. "I would have liked to have seen more."

"And afterwards?" Mrs. Poulet questioned. "You came straight home?"

"Yes, Mama," Roseanna responded. "Denis would have invited us to tea, but he had an engagement."

"I see," Mrs. Poulet mused. "You mentioned that Lord Czarski was with you."

Roseanna frowned as her mother used the formal mode of address, but she told herself that perhaps it was because Mr. Sandford, old stuffed shirt himself, was there.

"Yes, Mama," she murmured.

"You appear to be seeing a great deal of him," Mrs. Poulet remarked.

Roseanna started. "Do I?" she countered.

"We don't really," Evelina said.

"You always seem to talk of him," Mrs. Poulet commented.

"I was not aware of it," Roseanna prevaricated.

"If we have," Evelina pointed out, "it was only because he is staying with Denis, and whenever we meet, he makes up a foursome."

"Yes," Roseanna concurred. "They seem to be great friends."

"Indeed," Mrs. Poulet stated disapprovingly.

"Why do you say that?" Evelina demanded.

Mrs. Poulet shrugged. "It worries me," she answered.

"What worries you, Mama?" Roseanna wondered.

"Lord Czarski," Mrs. Poulet informed her.

Evelina's brows furrowed. "Marek?" she asked. "But why?"

"Because, apart from knowing he is Denis's friend," Mrs. Poulet replied, "I have no idea of who or what he is. Do you?"

"No, Mama," Roseanna returned. "Does it matter?"

Mrs. Poulet raised her eyebrows. "Of course it matters!" she exclaimed. "I cannot allow my daughter and my niece to be continually in the company of a man about whom no one knows anything!"

"But Denis—" Evelina began.

"Hrmph!" Mrs. Poulet snorted, cutting her short. "We can hardly go to him for information!"

"Why not?" Roseanna questioned innocently.

"Because it wouldn't do," Mrs. Poulet insisted flatly.

Roseanna and Evelina knew that tone. It didn't matter that it was perfectly possible to ask Denis and that he would not be offended, Mrs. Poulet had put her foot down and that was that.

"Perhaps, madam," Mr. Sandford suggested, "it may help if I made some inquiries about this Lord Czarski."

"What an excellent idea! It would certainly set my mind at rest!" Mrs. Poulet exclaimed. "But I would not wish to put you to any trouble."

"It would be no trouble, I assure you," Mr. Sandford responded. "Indeed, it would give me great pleasure."

"Would it?" Mrs. Poulet wondered coyly.

"Whatever I can do to ease your burdens does," Mr. Sandford told her.

"Thank you, sir," Mrs. Poulet breathed. "That is so very kind of you."

"Not at all," Mr. Sandford purred.

Roseanna and Evelina exchanged meaningful glances. First the dancing; then the sudden unannounced switch to half mourning; now this. Mrs. Poulet was coming to rely rather heavily on Mr. Sandford.

Roseanna and Evelina did not approve, but there was nothing they could do about it. Mr. Sandford was in an unassailable position. His character was above reproach, his manner was correct—even deferential.

No one had been able to find fault with him. And yet ... and yet ...

Roseanna sighed. Evelina, gauging the cause correctly, nodded slightly in acknowledgment. They could not fight his insidious and ever-increasing influence over Mrs. Poulet.

"What do you think Mr. Sandford will learn about Marek?" Roseanna queried, when they were alone.

"Nothing much," Evelina replied. "He seems a pretty straightforward character to me. No skeletons in the cupboard, if that's what you're worried about."

"Hmmmm," Roseanna mused.

The vision of Count Czarski's expression of hatred swam before her. Despite Evelina's assurances, she was not certain what Mr. Sandford would unearth if he really started digging.

A couple of days later, Mr. Sandford again visited them.

"I have the information you asked me to get," he announced.

"So soon!" Mrs. Poulet exclaimed. "How very clever of you!"

"Thank you," Mr. Sandford returned, almost, but not quite, blushing with pleasure.

"Excellent," Evelina stated. "Now you can put an end to Aunt's fears."

"Ahem!" Mr. Sandford cleared his throat uncomfortably.

Roseanna and Evelina stiffened. Whatever Mr. Sandford had discovered was definitely *not* going to allay Mrs. Poulet's anxieties.

"Would you like me to tell you now?" Mr. Sandford began. "Or ... ?"

"No!" Evelina interrupted. "Not now!"

The other three turned towards her.

"Why ever not, dear?" Mrs. Poulet asked, bewildered.

"If, as I suspect, you have learned something that is...not good, concerning Marek—" Evelina started.

"You are correct in that assumption," Mr. Sandford interposed.

"...then I do not think you should tell us," Evelina concluded, "unless he is present to explain it, and perhaps to defend himself."

A silence fell. Everyone waited to see what Mr. Sandford would say to that.

"Your niece is quite right, madam," Mr. Sandford stated. "In all fairness, Lord Czarski should be here to defend himself—"

"If necessary," Roseanna murmured.

"Er—quite so—if necessary," Mr. Sandford completed, "against the charges I am about to make."

Mrs. Poulet nodded in assent. "I shall send him a note at once!" she declared, rising and going to the escritoire.

In half a minute the missive was finished, and a footman was dispatched with it to the Albany.

"You have brought your daughter and your niece up well, madam," Mr. Sandford commented while they waited. "Their sense of justice does credit to you."

Mrs. Poulet smiled. "You are very kind, sir," she responded.

Roseanna remembered nothing of the rest of their tête-à-tête. Her heart was in her mouth. She did not know why, but she was frightened, not for herself, but for Count Czarski.

"What has Mr. Sandford found out about him?" she asked herself silently. "How bad is it? Can Marek explain it away? Will he be able to satisfy Mama?"

The seconds ticked away. It seemed an age to Roseanna, though in fact Count Czarski answered Mrs. Poulet's note promptly by appearing in person within thirty minutes. He was so gracious to Mrs. Poulet and to Mr. Sandford as he entered the house that they were both put to shame. But alas, they were undeterred.

"I...I am afraid," Mrs. Poulet said, fighting her embarrassment, "that we are here to discuss...a matter of—er—um—some gravity."

"So you wrote in your letter," Count Czarski stated. "You seemed to imply that my presence was required."

"That is correct," Mr. Sandford confirmed. "We—er—have something to—ahem!—put to you."

Count Czarski was still polite, but puzzled.

"I see," he answered. "Concerning what?"

Mrs. Poulet bit her lip. When she had requested Mr. Sandford to carry out his investigations, she had done so believing she had every right to pry into Count Czarski's life in order to protect her daughter. But the count's charm, coupled with his air of innocence, were forcing her to see her actions in a less-admirable light—and she hated him for that.

"Concerning yourself, Lord Czarski," she replied.

"Indeed?" Count Czarski questioned.

Still, he maintained the right mixture of bewilderment, friendliness, and deference. How dare he be so civilized! He made her feel such a fool!

"Mr. Sandford ... has discovered a few things ..." Mrs. Poulet continued awkwardly, "which ... so he tells us ... you should be here to ... to clarify ... if you—er—wish to do so."

Count Czarski was no longer smiling. He frowned, and his light brown eyes seemed to become brittle and bore into her.

"I do not follow you, madam," he said. He turned to Mr. Sandford. "Perhaps you would be good enough to enlighten me, sir."

Mr. Sandford bowed in acknowledgment. He, too, was uncomfortable. Count Czarski seemed so open, so frank—every inch a gentleman. Looking at him, one could not conceive that there was anything in his past to be ashamed of. Even so ...

"I shall certainly try," he answered stiffly.

"I am obliged to you," Count Czarski returned. "Pray proceed. I am all attention."

6

.Mr. Sandford cleared his throat. "When you were first introduced to this family," he began uneasily, "we—er—they assumed that you were Russian."

He paused awkwardly and looked at Count Czarski. The latter raised an eyebrow. His face hardened, but he made no comment.

"Er—we have since learned," Mr. Sandford proceeded, "or rather, *I* have since learned, that you are, in fact, Polish."

"That is correct," Count Czarski admitted. "I am."

"Ahem!" Mr. Sandford breathed significantly.

There you are, you see, he seemed to say. *You can't trust these foreigners.*

"I hope you do not imagine I intended to deceive you, madam." Count Czarski addressed Mrs. Poulet.

"Oh, no, indeed!" Roseanna answered for her mother.

Count Czarski gave a slight nod of his head, indicating his appreciation. Then he returned to Mr. Sandford.

"Had you ever mentioned that you thought I was Russian, either to myself or to Mr. Martin," he informed him, "you would naturally have been told that this was not so."

"Er—yes. Er—quite so," Mr. Sandford muttered.

An embarrassed silence fell. Then Mr. Sandford spoke once more.

"You are a prisoner of war, are you not?" he inquired.

There was a sharp intake of breath from the ladies, and all eyes were on Count Czarski.

"I am," he confirmed.

"Really?" Evelina questioned, interested. "When did you become one?"

"I was captured last autumn by the British," Count Czarski responded, "and brought to England. I gave my *parole* to Mr. Martin, and I am at present staying with him in his flat in the Albany."

As the discussion progressed, Mrs. Poulet's eyes widened with horror. A Pole! An ally of Napoleon's! An enemy of England's! A prisoner of war! Was this the sort of man who should be seen in company with her daughter and her niece?

"I think I am going to faint," Mrs. Poulet reflected to herself.

She closed her eyes and swayed where she sat, but the ladylike black oblivion would not come.

Count Czarski was aware that Mrs. Poulet disapproved of his nationality and status. He saw that Mr. Sandford looked quite grim and that Evelina was frowning as though she did not fully understand the reason for the fuss.

Count Czarski did not care what opinion they held. He was concerned with the reaction of one person only—Roseanna. He glanced at her and observed that she seemed ready to cry. Her eyes were pleading with him for some word, some explanation...

Normally, Count Czarski would have walked out of the house, dismissing Mr. Sandford and Mrs. Poulet as intolerant, impudent puppies, hardly worth troubling himself with. But there was Roseanna. For her sake he would endure this unwarranted attack; for her sake he was prepared to defend himself.

"I am afraid I fail to see why you should be shocked," Count Czarski stated.

"We did not know—" Mr. Sandford began.

"You could have learned this from Denis Martin," Count Czarski interrupted, "if you had but asked him. And since neither I nor anyone else conspired to misrepresent or conceal the facts from you, I cannot conceive why you are annoyed. Nor do I see why you are behaving as if you suspected I had done something reprehensible."

Roseanna gazed defiantly at Mr. Sandford. Count Czarski had echoed her thoughts. What would Mr. Sandford say—what could he say—to that?

"He can hardly blame Marek for his nationality," she told herself. "He had no choice about where he was born!"

"You are an enemy of England!" Mr. Sandford declared pompously. "Had you been Russian, as we supposed, we should have welcomed you with open arms as our dear ally in the struggle against the tyrant Bonaparte. But as a Pole..."

Hitherto Count Czarski had kept his temper in check, albeit with difficulty. But Mr. Sandford had gone too far. His fury could now no longer be contained.

Roseanna ached for him as she saw the color drain from his cheeks and noticed his hands clench so tightly that it seemed to her he would crush his own fingers into a pulp if he maintained his grip for much longer.

"Yes, I am a Pole," Count Czarski cut in. "And I thank God it is so and that I am *not* Russian!"

"Really, Lord Czarski, I—" Mr. Sandford started.

But Count Czarski was in no mood to permit him to finish.

"Do you know what Russia is today?" he demanded. "Do you know what it was in the past?"

"I don't see what history has to do with anything!" Mr. Sandford exclaimed.

But Count Czarski was not listening.

"Four hundred years ago, Russia was a petty, trifling, barbaric, puny, inconsequential duchy, consisting only of the territory encircling Moscow!" he informed them in ringing tones. "In those days Poland, my beloved Poland—and Lithuania together—stretched from the Oder to the Dnieper, from the Baltic to the Black Sea. Kiev, Riga, Minsk, and a thousand other cities you ignorant peasants imagine are Russian were Polish for centuries!"

"Oh!" Mrs. Poulet cried, coloring with anger. "That is most unfair! We are neither ignorant nor peasants!"

"Then why do you behave as if you were?" Count Czarski challenged.

Mrs. Poulet gave a gasp of indignation. She was so infuriated by this question that she could only splutter incoherently with rage. Her eyes besought Mr. Sandford to rescue her.

"I think, Lord Czarski, you must be mistaken," Mr. Sandford stated. "The cities you have named are Russian, not Polish. In fact," he added, pleased with himself for having recalled the information, "I believe that Kiev is known as the Mother of Russian Cities."

"Hah!" Count Czarski cried. "By whom? The Russians? Those liars forget that every inch of land from Smolensk west was originally Polish!"

"I won't quarrel with you," Mr. Sandford said.

"No doubt because you can't," Count Czarski retorted.

"I beg your pardon?"

"You won't quarrel with me because you are unable to, aren't you? I am right! Admit it! You know absolutely nothing about any country other than your own!"

"I . . ." Mr. Sandford could not continue. He was not able to refute the allegation.

"What do you know about my country, Mr. Russophile?" Count Czarski demanded. "Nothing! Isn't that so?"

"Er—well. I . . . er . . . that is . . ." Mr. Sandford stammered, wishing he could deny it.

"I thought so!" Count Czarski snapped. "Do you know how Poland, Lithuania, and Hungary combined to defend Christendom against the Turks? No. Do you know about the battle of Mohacs? No. Do you know how many of us died so that you could sleep safely in your beds? No. Well? I am correct—yes?"

"Er...now that you mention it," Mrs. Poulet assented, "no, we have not heard of any of this, but—"

"But?" Count Czarski cut in savagely. "If it had not been for Poland, for Lithuania, and for Hungary, the barbarian hordes from the East, the Turks and other tyrannical conquerors, would have overrun every square foot of Christian Europe. We saved you. And what thanks did we get for it?"

"None, by the sound of it," Evalina commented dryly.

"Precisely. None. You permitted this Russia, this wretched, corrupt Duchy of Moscovy to take first one piece and then another piece of our land," Count Czarski went on. "An abominable slave state was created, from which thousands upon thousands fled. And what did you do? You made treaties with it in the name of peace and free trade!"

"Come now, Lord Czarski..." Mr. Sandford tried to protest.

But Count Czarski was having none of it.

"This monstrosity that you call 'our dear ally' grew and grew," he continued. "Motivated by those twin evils, greed and fear, it spread its tentacles north, south, east, and west until there was nowhere for the downtrodden, the tortured, the wronged to flee to, no place of safety, no refuge anywhere."

As he paused for breath, Count Czarski's teeth bared into a snarl. He had the same expression of undying hatred that Roseanna had seen when he had gazed at the Grand Duchess of Oldenburg. She shivered as she watched him. Never had she seen such naked passion!

No one contradicted the count. No one had the power to utter a sound against him. They were all mesmerized.

"In the last century," Count Czarski proceeded, "Poland was stripped of everything. Europe chose to forget how we had once defended her. She closed her eyes to our plight. Our country was divided into portions and parceled out to other nations."

"There you are, then," Mr. Sandford said, finding

his voice momentarily. "It wasn't merely Russia. Austria and Prussia attacked you too."

"But Russia was the worst," Count Czarski insisted. "Warsaw, our glorious capital, became a mere Russian city. Poland ceased to exist. The Polish people became nothing. Do you know what it is for a freedom-loving nation to be crushed under the heel of tyranny? Can you even begin to imagine what it is like for those who are freeborn to be made slaves?"

Roseanna shook her head in negation.

Count Czarski continued to look at her as he went on speaking.

"When Napoleon came along and attacked Russia, I fought on his side," he stated in calmer tones than he had hitherto used. "Yes, I fought for my country's freedom. I chose to don a French uniform, not because I have any great love for Napoleon—or for France—but because I hoped to help liberate my people. I wanted to hear my children, my neighbors, my friends, my servants, the very dog in the street, respond to me in my own language instead of in Russian! I wanted to know that my country was prosperous, my people were happy, and that future generations would be free. I wanted to hear my countrymen laugh and sing and shout. I wanted joy instead of misery, pride instead of shame, autonomy instead of slavery."

A hugh fell when he ceased to speak. Mr. Sandford seemed slightly embarrassed, but whether by the words Count Czarski had uttered or by his un-English display of emotion was difficult to gauge. Mrs. Poulet was applying the smelling salts to herself. Evelina was interested but detached, and Roseanna was stunned.

Count Czarski himself was shaking with fury. His hands clenched and unclenched at his sides. He had stopped talking. He used the silence to catch his breath and to bring himself under control once more.

"I fail to see why what you have told us should alter anything," Mr. Sandford remarked coldly.

"Really? What would you have had me do?" Count Czarski sneered at him. "Fight for Russia, I suppose!"

"It would have been more acceptable," Mr. Sandford allowed.

Count Czarski gnashed his teeth. "You blame me because I did not wish to see my people crushed by tyranny? You condemn me because I did not want them to live under the yoke of slavery?" he demanded. "You find it reprehensible that I had no desire to witness my countrymen suffer under their new rulers? You consider it wrong that I objected to being governed by the Royal Bastards of Russia?"

Mrs. Poulet gave a cry of horror and put her hands over her ears. There was a hissing sound from Evelina, and Roseanna gasped.

Mr. Sandford's cheek twitched with anger.

"Lord Czarski," he exclaimed, "the Russian royal family are our allies and it behooves you to speak well of them!"

"Never!" Count Czarski retorted.

"Lord Czarski, the Czar of Russia is highly esteemed here," Mr. Sandford informed him patronizingly, "and the rest of the Romanov family—"

"They may call themselves Romanov but they are no more Romanov than you are," Count Czarski butted in. "Peter III, the last of the Romanovs, was incapable of fathering a child. And Catherine, his dear sweet ruthless German wife, used her body as a stepping-stone to the throne. Whose child Czar Paul was I do not know, but he was certainly not the offspring of Czar Peter!"

"Well!" Mrs. Poulet cried, shocked.

"The Romanov family is dead," Count Czarski went on, as if he had not heard her, "and those who sit in its place insult the name. And this mockery, this Czar Alexander, this descendent of a prostitute and her anonymous stud, are the rulers you wish my people and I to revere? Never!"

His voice rang out as he spoke. No one could refute his allegations, so they listened, appalled, as he continued.

"You find it unacceptable that I attempted to prevent this?" he questioned bitterly. "Oh, I was on the losing side, I admit that. I did make a mistake in not choosing the winners. Yes. I agree that was unpardonable. But what other course was open to me? Answer me that?"

No response.

"What would you have had me do?" Count Czarski persisted. "Grovel at the tyrants' feet? Throw my lot in with those who are draining the lifeblood of my country? Bow to the heir of a woman who was more rapacious than any whore of Babylon?"

Again there was no reply.

"Do you seriously imagine that I could have had any self-respect if I had ignored my people's needs?" Count Czarski asked them. "Do you really believe that I had any choice but to fight for my country? No, my friends. Mine was the only possible course. I would have been unable to live with myself if I had not endeavored to free my people."

"And now ... you have tried," Roseanna remarked hesitantly. "And you ... have failed."

Count Czarski looked straight into her eyes, and it seemed to her that his gaze softened.

"Yes," he answered. "I have tried and I have failed. Is that a crime?"

"N-n-no," Roseanna stammered. "But ... what are you going to do now? Return to ... to Poland?"

Count Czarski's expression became very sad.

"No," he told her. "I cannot go back."

"Wh-where will you go, then?" Roseanna asked.

"I shall emigrate as soon as peace is declared," he informed her. "I shall go to America and start my life there anew."

"That seems like running away," Mr. Sandford commented.

Count Czarski glared at him. "Does it?" he countered.

"To me," Mr. Sandford returned, "it does."

"Then all I can say, sir, is that you know precious little about me," Count Czarski declared, "or, for that matter, about life."

"You are being presumptuous!" Mr. Sandford accused.

"I disagree, sir," Count Czarski contradicted coolly. "It is you who have presumed, not I."

Mrs. Poulet viewed this as a criticism of herself as well as of Mr. Sandford.

"I think, Lord Czarski," she stated icily, "that you had better leave."

"At once, madam," Count Czarski concurred brusquely. "Good day."

He bowed and clicked his heels in the German fashion, then left the house, unceremoniously slamming the door behind him.

"Tsk-tsk," Mr. Sandford remarked. "There you are, you see. Now you know what he is really like!"

"Indeed I do!" Mrs. Poulet cried feelingly.

"A savage—an unrestrained savage!" Mr. Sandford exclaimed. "And an enemy of Britain!"

"What a good thing you looked into this for us!" Mrs. Poulet added. "Who would have guessed that he was such a monster?"

Roseanna burst into tears.

Evelina put her arms around her cousin.

"Don't cry, Roseanna," she comforted.

But Roseanna could not stem the flow.

"How that wretched man has upset poor Roseanna!" Mrs. Poulet declared. "What ever could Denis have been thinking of, letting them meet?"

"We all make mistakes," Mr. Sandford said magnanimously.

"Yes, and as soon as we discover them, we must do our best to correct them," Mrs. Poulet decided firmly. "Roseanna?"

"Yes, Mama?" Roseanna managed to respond.

"You must write to Lord Czarski at once and tell him that you never wish to see him again!" Mrs. Poulet informed her.

7

Roseanna gasped in horror. "I . . . I . . . c-can't" she stammered.

How could she say such a thing to the count? It wasn't true! Despite what Mr. Sandford had revealed, despite what her mother believed, Roseanna's feelings towards Count Czarski were unchanged.

"Of course you can," Mrs. Poulet returned, in her brisk, no-nonsense tone. "I shall compose the letter for you, never fear, and one of the servants can take it to the Albany."

"N-n-no!" Roseanna protested. "I—I c-can't!"

"Rubbish!" Mrs. Poulet retorted.

She opened the escritoire and brought out the paper and the ink.

Roseanna was helpless. It was no use her objecting any further. Mr. Sandford came to her side. He put his arm around her and assisted her to rise. Then he guided her to the chair in front of the writing table.

Roseanna was in a daze. She heard her mother's

voice dictating to her and somehow her fingers moved, taking down the words. It was like a bad dream, a hideous, twisted nightmare that had ensnared her and robbed her of power. She could not argue, she could not fight. Like a sleepwalker, she obeyed her mother's commands.

Roseanna had no idea what she wrote. She was far too upset to pay attention to what her mother was saying.

"If only I could stop crying!" she thought.

But her tears continued to flow, on and on, almost blinding her.

When the letter was finished, Mrs. Poulet seized it and read it eagerly through.

"Yes! Yes!" she declared with satisfaction. "That is perfect!"

"M-may I go to my room n-now?" Roseanna asked.

"Yes, of course," Mrs. Poulet replied.

Roseanna fled from the drawing room. She ran upstairs and flung herself down on her bed. There she wept as if her heart would break.

It seemed ages later when Evelina came up to tell Roseanna that it was time for dinner.

"Go away," Roseanna said brokenly.

"Come on, Roseanna," Evelina urged, "open up."

"No."

"You can't stay up here crying indefinitely. You'll ruin your eyes if you do."

Abruptly Roseanna sat up and surveyed herself in the mirror that stood over her dressing table. Her eyes were red and swollen. Her face was damp and distorted by her grief. Evelina was right—she had to get a grip on herself.

Roseanna came to the door and unlocked it.

"I've just seen myself in the looking glass," she commented. "I look terrible."

Evelina studied her cousin. "Yes, you do, don't you?" she agreed.

"Thank you!" Roseanna returned waspishly.

Evelina sighed. "I'm sorry about this, Roseanna,"

she stated. "I had no idea that you and he...that he meant anything to you."

Roseanna swallowed. "I...I like him," she murmured.

"Hmmmm. Ye-es."

Pause.

"What do you think he'll do...about that letter?" Roseanna asked.

Evelina shrugged noncommittally. "I have the faintest notion," she responded. "Frankly, everyone was so upset I hardly know what Aunt dictated."

"That makes two of us," Roseanna told her. "Oh, I do hope I won't have to wait long for the answer!"

Roseanna's wish was granted. Count Czarski's reply to the missive her mother had compelled her to send arrived the following morning. Roseanna was not allowed to see it, though. Mrs. Poulet appropriated it as the maid brought it in, and opened it at once. She then proceeded to read it aloud to the assembled company at the breakfast table, including Mr. Sandford.

Roseanna cringed inside.

Count Czarski was incredibly polite—and distant. He informed Roseanna that he quite understood. As peace was imminent, he would soon be emigrating to America in any case, and then she would no longer be troubled by his presence in her country.

"Nice enough, I suppose," Mrs. Poulet remarked, screwing up the letter and flinging it into the fire.

Roseanna stifled a cry of despair. His first letter to her! Even though the tone was so cold and so remote, she had wanted to keep it—badly. To see it consumed by the flames made her ache with misery.

"It was extremely courteous," Evelina commented.

"Yes, it was," Mrs. Poulet agreed. "I am certain that Denis helped him to compose it."

"Undoubtedly," Mr. Sandford concurred. "Lord Czarski would never have managed it on his own; he is far too uncouth!"

Roseanna's mouth turned down as she listened to them tearing Count Czarski's character to shreds.

"I never knew it was possible to be so unhappy!" she thought. "Why, oh why, couldn't they like him?"

Mrs. Poulet ignored Roseanna's wretchedness as much as she could. She regarded the whole incident as unfortunate but closed. And she was glad it was over. Naturally she was sorry that her daughter was upset, but she did not really understand why she should be.

When Mrs. Poulet asked him for his opinion, Mr. Sandford ventured to suggest that Roseanna had been shocked by the way Count Czarski had behaved. It never occurred to him that it was the manner in which he and her mother had handled the situation which distressed Roseanna.

"She'll cheer up now that her brothers are home for the holidays," Mrs. Poulet stated. "Won't she?"

"Of course she will," Mr. Sandford assented.

And besides having the company of her two younger brothers to brighten the scene for Roseanna over Easter, this year it was rather special: The war was over; peace had finally arrived in Europe.

For more than twenty years, battle after battle had been fought the length and breadth of the Continent. The flower of manhood had perished; the first flush of enthusiasm had long ago waned and in its place had grown bitter disillusionment.

People were heartily sick of the seemingly endless conflict, in England as well as everywhere else. They wanted the fighting to stop. They wanted a solution that did not cost more lives. Suddenly it came. Every newspaper in the land carried news of Napoleon's abdication at Fontainebleau. And London—nay, the world—went mad with joy.

How could Roseanna be gloomy? The whole country was deliriously happy. The illuminations in London alone lasted for three days. And this delight, this extra merrymaking, was in addition to the Easter festivities. Not only that, but her brothers were home for two whole weeks. What more could Roseanna desire?

But when she heard the news, when she learned that peace had been declared, Roseanna's heart sank. Peace meant that the count was no longer a prisoner of war. Peace meant that he was free. Peace meant that he would go away. Far away. His letter had said he would emigrate to America—a country so vast that once he arrived there it would be impossible for anyone, friend or foe, to trace him.

"I shall never see him again," Roseanna told herself.

She kept her true feelings hidden while her brothers were home. She pretended to be pleased that peace had finally come. She was genuinely glad to see her brothers, and because they enjoyed the celebrations so enthusiastically she did too. But once they had returned to school, her desolation was evident—even to her mother.

Though Mrs. Poulet could no longer ignore Roseanna's suffering, she was still completely unaware as to the cause. She assumed it was because Roseanna's brothers had had to go back to school. She believed that what Roseanna needed was a diversion—something to take her mind off their departure. Consequently, when Denis Martin, having returned to London from Gloucestershire, where he had been spending the holidays with his family, arrived at North Row unannounced, Mrs. Poulet was delighted.

"It is just the thing to bring the child out of herself," she reflected.

She smiled to herself. Secretly she had always hoped that Denis and Roseanna would fall in love and marry. She imagined that if they saw enough of each other they would realize that heaven had ordained it and it would not be long before he proposed and she accepted.

In consequence, since Mrs. Poulet desired this match above all else, she was prepared to do everything in her power to further the liaison. Thus it was that when Denis requested permission to speak to Roseanna *alone* that day, Mrs. Poulet readily assented.

"Ah! You've just reminded me!" she exclaimed. "Isn't that lucky!"

"Reminded you of what, Aunt?" Denis Martin inquired.

"Evelina mentioned earlier that she wanted to go shopping, because she had seen a few bargains in Oxford Street and if she waited until tomorrow it would probably be too late," Mrs. Poulet said. "Evelina, dear?"

"Yes, Aunt?" Evelina questioned. "Hello, Denis. I hope you are well."

"Hello, Evelina. Never felt better," Denis responded. "And you?"

"In excellent health, thank you."

"I hear you're going shopping this afternoon in Oxford Street."

Evelina frowned. "But I haven't got any m—" she began.

"Of course you have," Mrs. Poulet cut in before Evelina could protest that she had no money. "I told you I would give you five pounds. Here it is."

Evelina nearly fell down in astonishment. She thanked her aunt profusely and allowed herself to be bundled out of the house in the company of one of the maids and a footman.

Mrs. Poulet was pleased with herself. The rest of the servants were instructed to make themselves scarce. She herself decided to call on Mr. Sandford, and together they went for a drive in the park.

The way was now clear. The two cousins would be entirely alone in the house. They would be able to talk freely and without interruption.

Mrs. Poulet was certain that her labors would bear fruit.

Mrs. Poulet was positive that Roseanna and Denis would announce their engagement that afternoon. What was there to prevent it? Now that that dreadful Polish fellow had been removed and Roseanna had had a chance to see her cousin's true worth, and now that he realized what a lovely young lady she had become, there was bound to be a union between them.

However, while Denis was glad of the opportunity to talk to Roseanna on her own, romance was not exactly what he had in mind. He liked his cousin, but, though they were friends, there was nothing else between them as far as he was concerned.

Because he had never entertained any passionate
68

feelings for Roseanna, Denis had no idea of what Mrs. Poulet hoped would be the result of their talk. And even if he had known, he would not have proposed to Roseanna—then or ever.

As for Roseanna, she had no inkling of what had brought Denis to see her. She could not imagine why he paced up and down the drawing room impatiently, refraining from speaking a word as long as others were present.

But Denis Martin had his reasons. He kept himself in check until everyone else had departed. Then he rounded on Roseanna.

"What have you done to Marek?" he demanded angrily.

Roseanna backed away from his unexpected wrath.

"What do you mean?" she countered.

"You know what I mean!"

"I don't!"

"Oh, yes, you do!" he contradicted.

His face was grim. Roseanna had seen him in such a rage only once before. On that occasion he had lost his temper and struck one of the servants. He was older now; he had acquired greater self-control. But he was barely restraining himself from striking her, his own cousin.

Roseanna sensed that she was in danger and that she had to be careful not to provoke him.

"I don't know! I don't know!" she reiterated desperately. "What has happened? Why are you so cross with me?"

Denis Martin was livid. However, though he was seething with fury, he understood that Roseanna had told him the truth. He took a deep breath and walked away from her, fighting for composure.

"Perhaps," he said, speaking with difficulty, "I had better start at the beginning."

"It . . . it would be best," Roseanna agreed weakly.

She went to one of the armchairs and sank down in it.

"Do you remember when I was wounded?" Denis Martin questioned.

"About a year ago?" Roseanna asked. "Yes, I remember."

Denis seemed to relax slightly. "I was in hospital," he continued in calmer tones. "I and at least a thousand more: Swedish, Prussians, Russians, and English mainly, with a few others. One day, some French soldiers arrived with their colonel, who was seriously injured.

"Did their colonel . . . recover?" Roseanna prompted, as he stopped speaking.

"No. There was nothing the nuns could do for him. He was dead when he got there."

"Oh, dear. I am sorry."

"Not as sorry as we were."

"What do you mean?"

"Without their colonel, the French soldiers were completely undisciplined. They . . . I think they broke into the wine cellars . . . some of them were drunk," he went on. "But they were definitely shell-shocked and embittered, not only because their beloved colonel was dead but because they had lost battle after battle. They . . . they wandered through the hospital saying . . . heaven knows what . . . shouting slogans . . . As they did so, they learned the nationality of the wounded and consequently whose side we had been on. Once they discovered that, they . . . they started to kill us off."

Roseanna shuddered. "How awful!" she exclaimed.

"Pretty words," Denis sneered. "They don't give any sign you understand how horrible it was."

Roseanna did not reply. Better be quiet rather than risk antagonizing him when he was in this state.

"I could do nothing," Denis told her. "I was too weak to move. Most of the men there had been too seriously injured to be able to defend themselves. It's our way, you know. We soldiers tend to avoid hospitals. As long as we can walk, we—"

He stopped speaking and gnawed his lip for a second or two. Then he continued:

"We were helpless. Completely helpless. We could hear our comrades crying out as their arms, their legs, and their heads were hacked to pieces. Those screams...I shall never forget those screams. ...They haunt me waking and sleeping. I..."

Again he paused, then swallowed uncomfortably before he proceeded:

"All I could do—all any of us could do—was to lie there and wait our turn to be chopped to bits."

Roseanna felt sick. Her face had gone white and it took a great effort for her to stop herself from fainting.

"What...happened?" she inquired.

"Marek came along," Denis answered tersely.

"Pardon?"

"Marek came along," Denis repeated. "Somehow—don't ask me how—he stopped the massacre. And today there are more than eight hundred men who owe their lives to him. Do you wonder that I invited him to come here to me if ever he were taken prisoner? Are you surprised that I requested the War Office to put him on parole to me?"

"No," Roseanna responded, lowering her gaze so that she did not have to face his condemning eyes. "Please...go on."

"After the fall of Poland, during some insignificant skirmish between those French soldiers who tried to murder us in our beds and whom he now commanded and our own troops, Marek was taken prisoner," Denis stated. "He appealed to me and I used my influence to have him sent here."

Another silence, while Denis Martin searched for the right words, followed.

"Marek was so unhappy about what was going on in his country," Denis continued, "that I thought he would end his life. He had fought so desperately for Poland's freedom and now he saw it under the Russian yoke once more. Worse still, he can never return home, because the Russians, our dear allies, will kill him as surely as I stand here."

"Oh, no!" Roseanna exclaimed.

"You doubt it?" Denis questioned. And then, without waiting for her to answer, he went on: "They accused his younger brother of treason and had him beaten with the knout to make him confess. Can you imagine how you would feel if John or Michael were stretched out on the rack and whipped to death—"

"To death?" Roseanna interposed weakly.

"To death," Denis confirmed. "It doesn't take many strokes of the knout to kill, you know."

"Oh," Roseanna murmured, at a loss for something to say.

"Before Marek's family knew that his brother was dead, Marek's father went to the prison where he was incarcerated to try to save him. He was arrested, charged with complicity, and shot," he continued. "His mother traveled to Moscow to plead with the Czar for mercy for her husband and her son. She was sentenced to seven years hard labor, in Siberia. She died of cold and hunger on the way there. It's unbelievable, isn't it? All this because of a phantom plot, a crime that never was, a misinterpreted sentiment uttered by a poetic youth who loved his country!"

Roseanna gave an agonized cry and buried her head in her hands as if to shut out the horrifying scene Denis had depicted for her.

"Shall I go on?" Denis asked.

Roseanna nodded dumbly in assent.

"Marek sent his younger brothers and his sister out of the country," Denis told her. "And it was only just in time. There is a price on his head. If the Russians ever get hold of him, he can expect much the same fate as his brother or his parents."

"Oh, no!" Roseanna whispered.

Denis Martin gave her a minute to recover her composure before he spoke again.

"Marek is my friend and I am proud of that friendship," he stated. "I could not have a better, truer one. You know, he has saved my life more than once, and yet . . ."

His voice trailed off.

Roseanna stared at Denis. "More than once"? Of course! That was why he had wanted her to take his letter to Count Czarski. The latter had already rescued him from the jaws of death on one occasion—that was why Denis trusted him!

"Does Mama know?" Roseanna wondered silently. "Would it make any difference if she did?"

"You said that you thought Marek would end his life," Roseanna recalled suddenly.

"Yes," Denis confirmed.

"Then why did he bother with parole?"

"He did that chiefly as a matter of form," Denis explained. "He didn't care a jot about it for himself. He did it more for his servant's sake—the old Pole he has with him, who follows him everywhere like a faithful dog. You know the one I mean?"

"Yes."

"He felt conditions might be better for the old man."

"Oh."

"As I mentioned," Denis reminded her distractedly, "when I brought Marek to the Albany he didn't seem to mind whether he lived or died. Poland was everything to him. He dreamt of freeing his country. When the dream was shattered . . . so was he."

Roseanna frowned. She found it hard to conceive of anyone being so passionately fond of the land where they were born. And yet she knew it was true. She had only to recollect how Count Czarski had talked of his country to appreciate how much it meant to him.

But what was Denis saying now? Roseanna could hardly believe she was hearing him aright.

"And then he met you," Denis informed her. "I saw the change in him when . . . when we met in France. The old Marek was back. The panache. The devil-may-care . . ." He stopped speaking for a split second before he added, "Marek pretended he had had orders from the Emperor himself to move me to Paris. That's how he got me out of Craonne."

"He did that?" Roseanna gasped. "But . . . if they had caught him . . . he might have been . . . killed!"

"Yes," Denis concurred ruthlessly. "He could have been shot as a traitor by the French for endeavoring to assist me, or by the British as an escaped prisoner. You cannot conceive the risk he ran or the danger he was in. He laid his own life on the line to save mine—

for the second time! Can you understand why I value his friendship so highly?"

Roseanna's mouth was dry. The thought of what might have happened to Marek if . . . if anything had gone wrong! It was an effort even to utter one syllable.

"Yes," she managed to answer.

"Good. Now, where was I? Ah yes. Even in France, after you two had met for the first time, I saw that there was a change in Marek," he continued. "He . . . he had come alive. There is no other way to describe it. And I was glad for him."

"How . . . how did you know . . . it was because of me?" Roseanna questioned.

"I didn't. Not then. But I was happy for him whatever the cause," Denis replied. "It wasn't until we returned to London, when he danced with you at your coming-out ball, that I realized it was due to you. And I was doubly delighted."

Roseanna blinked in surprise. "You . . . you were?" she queried.

Dennis Martin nodded in assent. "You gave Marek a reason for living," he answered. "By introducing you to him I felt I had repaid at least part of the debt I owed him."

"I see," Roseanna murmured.

"Do you? Then why . . . ?"

"Yes?"

Denis Martin paced the floor.

"Because of some silly quarrel between the two of you . . . you have destroyed this new hope of his," he went on disjointedly. "You . . . you might just as well have stabbed him!"

8

Roseanna gave a cry of dismay. "No!" she exclaimed. "It is not true!"

"It is true!" Denis Martin retorted. "You have been playing with Marek's feelings and I would like to ... to wring your stupid little neck!"

Roseanna was hardly aware of her cousin's insulting words. She was far too upset by his unjust accusation.

"No! No!" she protested. "I haven't been playing with Marek's feeling! Truly I have not!"

"Haven't you?" Denis challenged.

"No!"

"In that case," he returned evenly, "perhaps you would be so kind as to tell me what has been going on."

Roseanna shivered apprehensively.

"Mama ... Mama considered that I—that we—had been seeing a great deal of Marek," she began, referring to Evelina and herself. "She ... she said that we spoke of him often. She ... she thought she ought to know more about him than the mere fact that he was staying with you."

"I agree," Denis stated. "Aunt should have known more than that. But why didn't she ask Marek? Or me? Either one of us could have given her whatever information she wanted."

"I know. I know. Evelina raised the same question. But Mama...Mama flattened her. She...she told her that she could not go to you. She wouldn't let us mention it to you either."

"Why not, pray?"

"Mama did not say why not. She simply indicated that the subject was closed."

"Indeed!"

"Look, Denis, I...I...it didn't seem important to me to wonder about Marek. I thought that since he was your friend, and you had allowed us to meet, that he must be respectable. I didn't need to know any more."

"I see. But Aunt did."

"Yes."

"I fail to understand why she would not come to me," Denis complained. "What did she imagine she would learn from other sources that she could not have discovered from her own nephew?"

Roseanna shrugged. "I have no idea," she answered. "I only know that Mr. Sandford offered to check on Marek for her, and she accepted."

"Did she!" Denis Martin was grim.

"Yes. And a couple of days later Mr. Sandford visited us and informed us that he had learned something bad about Marek."

"Really!"

"Yes. He...he wanted to tell us then and there, but Evelina insisted that we send for Marek so he could defend himself...if necessary."

"Good for Evelina! Why wasn't I summoned too?"

"You had already left for Gloucestershire by then."

"Hmmmmm. So Marek came round on his own, did he?"

"That's right."

"What then?"

76

"Mr. Sandford said that Marek was Polish—not Russian, as we had assumed—and that he was a prisoner of war."

"*I* could have told you that."

"Mr. Sandford made out that Marek was our enemy because he fought for Napoleon."

"Hrmph!" Denis snorted. "How did Marek take that?"

"N-n-not very well. He . . . he listened for a bit and then he pointed out that he had never kept his nationality a secret—"

"True," Denis Martin interposed.

"—and that he had fought for his country's freedom."

"Also true."

"Then he insulted the Russian royal family."

Denis laughed. "He's not very keen on them," he stated, "but that's nothing to get upset about, is it?"

Roseanna shook her head in negation. She was nearly in tears now, and finding it more and more difficult to speak.

"Go on!" Denis exhorted. "Don't stop there, for heaven's sake!"

"Mr. Sandford and Mama both said that Marek was being presumptuous and that he was an enemy of England. When he had gone they called him a savage and they told me I had to write to him informing him that I never wished to see him again."

Denis Martin drew in his breath. "Did they indeed?" he inquired. "And what, precisely, did you put in your letter?"

"I don't know."

"What!"

"I was so unhappy. I couldn't s-s-stop c-crying," Roseanna explained. "Mama made me . . . do it. . . . She dictated something. . . . The letter was sent. . . . And the next day Marek replied. Mama read his answer aloud at breakfast. Mr. Sandford was there. I could have died! Then . . . then she threw it into the fire."

Denis whistled. "So!" he hissed. "That's the way the land lies, is it?"

Roseanna stared at him. Her desire to weep had suddenly vanished.

"What are you talking about?" she asked.

"Listen, Roseanna," Denis responded, "I have had my suspicions concerning our precious Mr. Sandford for some time."

"Suspicions?"

"Yes. I believe that he wants to marry your mother and that ever since your father's accident he has been doing what he can to get into her good graces."

"I've noticed he is fond of her, but . . ."

"But?"

"Would he go so far as to blacken Marek's name? Would Mama want him to do that? Consider, even you agreed that we did not know much about him."

"That's not the point."

"Pardon?"

"*Yes*, he would try to slander Marek, and *yes*, your mother did want him to," Denis Martin told her.

"But why?"

"Don't you see? Aunt wants *us* to marry!"

Roseanna frowned. "Us?" she echoed.

"You and I."

"Not Marek and I?"

"Definitely not."

"I . . . I don't understand."

"As far as dear Auntie is concerned, you and I ought to marry," he clarified. "In her view, you were paying far too much attention to Marek. You were being led astray, deviating from the true purpose of those meetings she worked so hard to arrange for us."

"Like the Frost Fair?"

"Exactly. And the Grand Duchess of Oldenburg's arrival in London."

"Oh."

"As far as she could see, Marek was an obstacle and she had to remove him," Denis Martin concluded. "That's why she couldn't ask me about him. She suspected that I would paint him in glowing colors to you."

"Would you have?"

"Naturally. How could I do otherwise? I admire him enormously and I am deeply indebted to him. Aunt sensed that, and she knew it would not do. You had to

78

be made to hate Marek. So she put it to Mr. Sandford, and he, cunning wretch, understood immediately."

"But what he learned about Marek is the same as what you told me," Roseanna protested. "There is nothing bad in his past, is there?"

"Certainly not."

"But ..."

"Don't you see?"

"No."

"It was not a question of finding out more about Marek than I could tell them, but of reinterpreting the facts, of proving that Marek was no good," Denis explained. "Mr. Sandford had to show everything in as unfavorable a light as possible. He had to vilify Marek—to his face if necessary. Then, when they had finished with Marek and succeeded in putting his back up, they started on you. Aunt composed that letter knowing what Marek would reply—by the way, what did he reply?"

"N-n-nothing much. He said that he understood and that he would be emigrating soon, so I would not be troubled by his presence any more."

"There you are! Precisely what Aunt and Mr. Sandford had been hoping for! Together they had achieved their object, which was to cut Marek out of your life. Do you follow?"

Roseanna considered her cousin's theory. Suddenly everything made sense. Her mother's anxiety lest Denis Martin had been killed in France. Her great joy when he had appeared at Roseanna's coming-out ball. Mrs. Poulet's overwhelming disappointment when she learned that Denis would be spending Easter in Gloucestershire instead of in London.

At last Roseanna perceived why her mother had always acquiesced so readily to her own and Evelina's requests to go out whenever they had Denis Martin as their escort. Mrs. Poulet's rage and her unreasoned attack on Count Czarski were also comprehensible.

"And now I suppose Aunt has left us alone because she thinks I am going to ask you to marry me," Denis stated, breaking the silence.

"But I don't want to marry you!" Roseanna gasped.

Denis laughed. "Thank heavens for that!" he declared. "*I* don't want to marry you either."

"That's a fine thing to say!" Roseanna cried perversely.

Denis grinned at her. "It's just as well that neither of us intends to wed the other, isn't it?" he questioned.

"I . . . I suppose so," Roseanna conceded.

"However," he continued, "it does not alter the fact that your mama has got it into her head that we are made for each other."

"But why?" Roseanna wailed.

"I have no idea," Denis replied. "She believes it is for the best, no doubt."

Roseanna sighed. "Oh, what am I to do?" she inquired forlornly.

"What are *you* to do?" Denis Martin countered. "What are *we* to do, surely?"

"What do you mean?"

"Well, my dear cousin, if we do not act quickly, then Aunt will maneuver me into having to propose to you, and you will be compelled to accept," he explained. "We shall be married within a month—"

"—and tied to each other for life," Roseanna completed.

"Good Lord! What a horrible thought!"

Roseanna pouted. "I don't think I like your inference, Denis," she stated primly.

"Pardon?"

"It seems to me that whereas you have always said you liked me, in fact you do not."

"Roseanna, you can be most provoking. Of course I like you. But liking you and loving you are two different things. And I certainly do not intend to marry you."

"As you said earlier, my dear cousin, thank heavens for that."

Denis grew serious.

"We must plan our next move very carefully," he warned her. "There isn't room for any mistakes."

"Point taken."

"First, you must not let Aunt know how long I have

been here," he informed her. "Tell he that I only stayed for a minute—or less."

"Oh? Why?"

"Because otherwise she is going to insist that I proposed to you and we shall have the devil of a job trying to convince her that I didn't."

"Oh."

"Next, we have to get you out of the house so you can meet Marek secretly and convince him that it wasn't your idea to send him that letter."

"But how?" Roseanna demanded. "I never go out alone. Either I am with Evelina or my maid or you. I—"

"Didn't I say we had to be careful?"

"Yes, you did."

"Well, then."

Denis Martin paced up and down the room once more, frowning with concentration.

Roseanna watched his progress for several seconds before she spoke.

"When are we going to carry out this plan?" she questioned.

"As soon as possible."

"Hmmmmm."

"What is it?"

"Nothing. I was only thinking that Evelina told me she wanted to see Mr. Town's paintings on velvet in New Bond Street," Roseanna remarked. "She also hoped to have a look at that new painting they are showing in Leicester Square."

"*The Battle of Vitoria?*"

"That's right. Now, if you had come to invite us both to see those things with you tomorrow, Mama would say yes," Roseanna commented. "Then I could visit Marek while you two went first to New Bond Street and then to Leicester Square. Before we returned to North Row, Evelina could tell me what it was like so that I could answer Mama's inquiries, and—"

"—and no one the wiser!" Denis Martin exclaimed, rubbing his hands with glee. "An excellent idea!"

Not only would it provide a cover for Roseanna's secret meeting with Count Czarski, but it also explained Denis Martin's own brief presence at the Poulet house in such a way that neither Mrs. Poulet nor Mr. Sandford would be able to refute it.

"It's perfect!" Denis Martin cried. "But will Evelina help?"

Roseanna's brows furrowed thoughtfully. "She might," she replied. "We are quite close, and I know she doesn't dislike Marek because of his nationality."

"Good. Ask her, then."

"Oh, yes. I shall certainly do that."

"Splendid. Let's set it for tomorrow. You tell Aunt that I invited you and Evelina out, and get her permission to go," Denis said. "Next, you enlist Evelina's assistance. If she consents, I shall take her to view both the paintings on velvet and *The Battle of Vitoria*, while you are at the Albany with Marek. We'll collect you before lunch. Evelina will tell you what the morning was like. Then we'll return to North Row and Aunt won't suspect a thing."

"But what if Evelina doesn't agree?"

"We shall have to find another way."

"And what if someone sees me going into the Albany and tells Mama?"

"Don't be silly."

"I am not being silly," Roseanna retorted. "You know what people in North Row are like!"

"Even if someone does see you, they won't necessarily know who you are, and they certainly won't guess that you weren't supposed to be there," Denis returned. "If worst comes to worst, you could always tell Aunt that you went into the Albany for a minute to get something, couldn't you?"

"Hmmmmm. Yes. I suppose so," Roseanna stated. "But . . . ?"

"But?" Denis Martin prompted.

"What if Marek won't listen to me?"

"Make him listen!"

"How?" Roseanna wanted to know.

"You're a woman, aren't you?" Denis cried in exasperation. "You have feminine wiles, don't you? Well, use them!"

"Really, Denis!" Roseanna complained. "You can be most deflating!"

"Only because you raise such ridiculous objections, my dear Roseanna. Now, have you got that? Is everything clear?"

"Crystal clear, except..."

"What's the matter now?"

"What if Marek won't see me, when you tell him about my visit?" Roseanna wondered.

9

Denis Martin sighed and raised his eyes to the heavens. And then, being answered, proceeded thus:

"I am not going to tell Marek."

"Not going to tell Marek?" Roseanna repeated.

"No. It will be a surprise."

"But . . . supposing he is out?"

"He won't be."

"Why not?"

"Because I say he won't be, that's why not!"

"But . . . ?"

"Now don't ask me any more questions—provoking girl!" Denis Martin exclaimed.

"Why not?"

"Because I have no time to answer them. I have to leave this minute. If I don't, Aunt will catch me here when she returns and she will know that I have stayed longer than you are going to tell her I did."

"Oh."

"Good-bye," Denis said. "Don't forget our plan."

"No. I won't," Roseanna responded. "Good-bye, then."

Roseanna gazed after Denis as he walked quickly from the house to the road. Within a few seconds he had disappeared from view.

Roseanna remained where she was, looking out of the window, imagining him hurrying towards the Albany.

"He doesn't want to be seen by Mama or by Mr. Sandford or by Evelina," she reflected.

That meant he would have to leave North Row as soon as he could. Perhaps he would nip down the alleyway that joined North Row to Green Street. From there he could avoid the main thoroughfares until he came to Upper Grosvenor Street. Then it was only a short distance across South Audley Street and into Adam's Mews.

"He'll be almost home by then," she thought.

She kept an anxious watch, counting the minutes from the time Denis Martin left her until Mrs. Poulet and Mr. Sandford arrived.

Suddenly she spotted them at the gate. Evelina was with them.

Roseanna glanced at the clock. Fifteen minutes had elapsed. Long enough for Denis to have made good his escape. She smiled and came onto the front steps to meet them.

"I met Aunt just as I was turning into George Street, so I got a lift home," Evelina greeted her. "Was that not fortunate?"

"Very," Roseanna agreed. "Did you buy anything?"

"Did I not!" Evelina declared excitedly. "I spent ever such a lot of money. Come inside. You must see!"

The maid and the footman who followed Evelina up the garden path were almost submerged by a sea of parcels, which bore silent witness to the success of her shopping expedition.

"Before you look at what Evelina has bought, Roseanna," Mrs. Poulet said, "there is something I want to ask you."

Roseanna, in the act of reentering the house, paused. "Yes, Mama?" she inquired.

"Did Denis have anything interesting to say?"

"Yes, he did," Roseanna answered brightly. "He invited Evelina and me to come to view Mr. Town's paintings on velvet in Bond Street and also *The Battle of Vitoria* in Leicester Square with him tomorrow."

"How lovely!" Evelina exclaimed. "I've been wanting to see both those things for ages. Do let us go, Aunt!"

"We'll see," Mrs. Poulet prevaricated. "Didn't he say anything else?"

"No, Mama," Roseanna responded.

Mrs. Poulet was evidently disappointed.

"Are you sure?" Mr. Sandford pressed.

"Quite sure, sir," Roseanna replied. "There wasn't time, you see."

"What do you mean?" Mr. Sandford queried.

"He only stayed a minute," Roseanna lied. "He had an appointment, I believe. Anyway, he was definitely in a hurry."

"Oh," Mr. Sandford murmured.

Mrs. Poulet's mouth turned down.

"Then why did he make such a point of seeing you on your own?" Mr. Sandford questioned.

Roseanna was annoyed with him for that.

"He wanted to know if I was really interested," she answered, indicating by her expression that she did not consider it any of his business.

"I see." Mr. Sandford was a little abashed.

"I told Denis I thought you would let us both go," Roseanna informed her mother.

"We can go, can't we, Aunt?" Evelina pleaded.

Mrs. Poulet managed a smile. "Yes, of course," she made herself respond, as she followed them into the house.

But she was puzzled. She sensed that Roseanna was withholding something from her. However, she could not fathom what it might be.

"Are you sure he didn't say anything else?" she persisted.

Roseanna lowered her eyes. She felt guilty about not telling the truth, but she knew that it was necessary—just this once.

"Quite sure, Mama," she said.

Then she proceeded upstairs to where Evelina and her maid were unpacking the purchases. When the maid had been dismissed and the two of them were alone, Evelina turned to her cousin.

"What have you and Denis been up to?" she demanded.

"Up to?" Roseanna countered innocently.

"Yes, *up to,*" Evelina repeated.

"Nothing."

"Hrmph!" Evelina snorted. "Well, maybe Denis isn't concocting anything, but I could have sworn that you had been up to something."

"How can you say such a thing?"

"Easily. I know you, Roseanna Poulet. I know what it means when you have that certain look in your eye."

Roseanna bit her lip. "Oh, dear. Do you think Mama has noticed?" she wondered.

"Oh, no. She hasn't the least suspicion."

"Are you sure?"

"Positive. Otherwise she would have catechized you as I am going to," Evelina assured her cousin. "Why? What's happened?"

Roseanna made a clicking noise with her tongue.

"I can't tell you."

"Why not?"

"Someone might overhear us."

Evelina shrugged. "Please yourself," she stated.

"Don't be offended."

"I am not," Evelina replied in her most affronted tones. "If you don't want to trust me with your secrets, then that is up to you."

"But I do trust you."

"Funny way you have of showing it."

"I'll tell you as soon as I can."

"When will that be?"

"Tomorrow morning when we meet Denis."

"Ah, so I was right! You are in collusion!"

"Yes."

Evelina frowned. "You're not planning to elope with him, are you?" she queried.

Roseanna laughed. "Good heavens, no!" she cried.

"That's all right, then. You had me worried for a moment. Very well. I'll wait until tomorrow."

"Good." Pause. "Evelina?"

"Yes?"

"I ... We ... need your help."

"Pardon? But ..."

"Please say you will agree to help us."

"Yes, of course I shall, " Evelina answered. "But ... what do I have to do?"

"Nothing, really, and certainly not yet," Roseanna replied. "Just be happy that we are going out with Denis tomorrow."

"You are being very mysterious."

"Am I?"

"Yes."

"Sorry."

Evelina studied her cousin thoughtfully.

"I won't have to miss the paintings on velvet or *The Battle of Vitoria*, will I?" she wanted to know.

"Oh, no. I promise you'll see them both."

"Splendid," Evelina responded.

The following morning, Denis Martin arrived to collect Roseanna and Evelina. He instructed his coachman to drive in the direction of Leicester Square, but as soon as they were out of sight of North Row, he changed his orders and told the man to proceed to the Albany.

Evelina was puzzled by the change in their itinerary. She turned to her cousin for an explanation.

"I am going to meet Marek today," Roseanna answered Evelina's unspoken query.

"What!" Evelina gasped. "You're not!"

"She is," Denis confirmed.

"Oh, Roseanna!" Evelina cried. "How could you!"

"You said you'd help us," Roseanna reminded her.

"I shall. I shall. But if Aunt ever gets wind of this . . ." Evelina began.

"She won't," Denis vowed. "Not if you are willing to assist us."

"But how?" Evelina inquired. "You know what she's like. We can't keep anything secret from her. We aren't going to lie to her—are we?"

"Yes," Denis admitted.

Evelina's hand flew to her mouth.

"I don't like it either," Roseanna stated, coloring, "but Mama has made it impossible for us to be frank with her."

"What do you mean?" Evelina demanded.

Briefly Denis Martin explained that he believed that Mrs. Poulet wanted him to marry Roseanna. In order to achieve her objective, she had cajoled Mr. Sandford into having Count Czarski investigated and into reinterpreting the facts to make them appear worse than in fact they were.

"She has been dishonest with all of us," Denis informed Evelina. "But we are onto her now, and we are not going to permit her to manipulate us any more."

Evelina listened attentively. When he concluded, she said:

"You could be right. Aunt has been far more eager to see the two of you together than she has been to see Roseanna in the company of other men."

"The trouble is, we don't want to marry," Denis Martin stated.

"It isn't that we don't like each other," Roseanna clarified hastily, "merely that we don't feel we are suited."

"Precisely," Denis Martin confirmed.

"I am with you there," Evelina remarked. "You two would be miserable together."

"So you see," Denis explained, "the only way to get out of this mess is to use subterfuge."

"Hmmmmm," Evelina murmured noncommittally.

"By being so nasty to Marek," Roseanna pointed out, "Mama and Mr. Sandford have made him believe that I don't want to see him again ever."

89

"But that is not true, is it?" Evelina asked.

"No," Roseanna answered. "It isn't."

"And it has made Marek very unhappy," Denis added.

"And me too," Roseanna commented.

"Hmmmmm," Evelina mused once more.

"We feel we must sort things out now," Roseanna told her, "before they get any worse."

Evelina considered the position carefully before she made up her mind.

"I agree," she decided eventually. "But I still don't understand how you imagine you can get away with deceiving Aunt."

Denis and Roseanna delineated their plan.

As Evelina heard them out, her eyes grew as round as saucers.

"I never knew the pair of you could be so devious!" she exclaimed.

Roseanna blushed.

"What do you think of it?" Denis questioned.

"It'll do," Evelina replied.

"You'll help us, then?" Roseanna queried.

"Certainly," Evelina answered.

"Splendid!" Denis declared. "We'll leave Roseanna at the Albany, then we'll go on to Leicester Square and New Bond Street."

"Wonderful!" Evelina cried.

By then they were almost at the Albany. Denis Martin ordered the carriage to stop and helped Roseanna to descend.

"We'll come back for you at half past twelve," he announced.

"Fine," Roseanna returned. "I shall be here."

She knew without his saying so that setting her down there was one extra little precaution. Hurriedly she walked the last few steps to the entrance of the Albany, where the porter admitted her. Then she almost ran to Denis's apartment.

Roseanna was terrified that she would not find Count Czarski there, although Denis Martin had repeatedly assured her she would. Her heart was in her mouth as she knocked on the door.

After what seemed to her an eternity, it opened and Count Czarski stood before her. When he saw her in front of him, his eyes widened with surprise and shock.

"Your cousin is not at home," he stated in a cold, unemotional voice.

Roseanna's heart was pounding. Her hands were trembling. Her mouth was dry. She tried to smile at him, but her own nervousness, coupled with his icy manner, made it impossible. All she could do was stare at him like an idiot.

"He went out earlier," Count Czarski added, when she failed to respond.

"I...I...I know," Roseanna managed to stammer. "May I...come in?"

Count Czarski stepped aside to admit her.

"You wish to wait for him here?" he questioned as he ushered her into the sitting room.

His politeness was faultless, and yet there was something about his behavior that made Roseanna shiver apprehensively.

"Denis was right," she thought.

The letter her mother had compelled her to write had wrought a terrible change in the count.

"N-no," she replied uncertainly. "I...I w-wanted to talk to you."

Count Czarski stiffened. His apparent indifference hurt Roseanna. In another moment she felt she would burst into tears.

"I must not," she insisted silently.

It was difficult enough for her to speak, as it was. If she wept, she would be totally unable to do so, and then she could not clear up the misunderstanding. There could be no further delay where that was concerned. It had to be dealt with...now!

Count Czarski closed the sitting-room door with a violent snap that made Roseanna jump.

"Won't you sit down?" he invited.

"Thank you," Roseanna heard herself return.

She lowered herself onto the edge of one of the upright gilt chairs that stood almost in the center of the room.

"How may I assist you?" Count Czarski inquired frostily.

Roseanna wrung her hands. Never had she been made to feel so unwelcome!

"It...it's about m-my letter," she murmured. "It may have been...unclear."

"I found it perfectly intelligible," Count Czarski assured her.

"I fear it may have been...misconstrued."

"I doubt it."

"Oh dear," Roseanna thought. "What am I to do?"

Count Czarski broke the silence:

"I understand from your letter that you did not wish to see me again," he stated. "Ever. What could be more lucid than that?"

"Mama made me write that letter," Roseanna answered. "It wasn't my idea. I...I don't even remember...I don't even know what was in it."

Until then, Count Czarski had stood in front of her, gazing at her with an expression which was reminiscent of someone finding an adder in a teapot. Now, abruptly, he moved away from her, toward the window overlooking the narrow lane that ran in between the conglomeration of apartments for young gentlemen of which the Albany was composed, so that he had his back to her.

"Did...Mrs. Poulet...dictate that note... to you?" he asked in a strangled voice.

"Yes," Roseanna responded.

Count Czarski neither spoke nor deigned to look at her.

Roseanna did not know what to do. She waited, still perched on the edge of her chair, twisting her hands this way and that.

"If only he would shout at me," she reflected. "If only he would rant and rage, I could bear it!"

But this refusal to utter a sound, this eerie quiet, was almost intolerable.

At last, at long last, Count Czarski turned his head halfway toward her so that he could just see her.

"You said in your letter," he informed her, "or rather, your mother did, that your family could not
92

entertain any enemies of this country in your house. Do you recollect that?"

"No," Roseanna answered.

"What do you recall of it?"

"Nothing."

"Nothing?"

The question was softly uttered. But the implication—the disbelief—was plain enough.

Roseanna swallowed. This was even worse than she had anticipated.

"Nothing," she reiterated. "I was so upset I hardly knew what I was doing. But if that is what Mama made me write, then...then it is not true."

"No?"

"No. We are not like that. At least," Roseanna corrected, "we weren't when Papa was alive."

Count Czarski did not miss the wistful tone in her voice. He remembered that when he had first been introduced to Mrs. Poulet she was in full mourning.

"When did your father die?" he asked.

"Nearly two years ago," she responded sadly, lowering her eyes.

Her lips trembled. It was as much as she could do to stop herself from crying when she thought about it. No. Mr. Poulet would not have insulted Count Czarski. He would have listened to his reasons for fighting on Napoleon's side against the Czar. And he would probably have agreed with them.

Another silence had fallen, and after a little while Roseanna glanced up at the count once more.

He was still by the window, but he was facing her fully now. As their eyes met, he leaned back slightly, gripping the edge of the windowsill with his hands.

There was a difference in his expression now, a searing pain, which Roseanna wished she could soothe away. She wanted to put her arms around him and comfort him. She rose to her feet and took half a step toward him. Then something in his countenance altered. It was very subtle, the merest trifle, but it was sufficient to warn her to stay where she was.

Roseanna bit her lip. She understood that he wanted

to believe her when she claimed that the letter had not been composed by her. But he did not dare.

Roseanna felt unaccountably weak. She swayed and put her hand on the back of the chair to steady herself.

"Of course," she continued hesitantly, "it was a shock when I . . . when we . . . found out you were Polish, especially as I . . . we . . . had presumed you were Russian."

"Indeed?" Count Czarski countered sarcastically.

Roseanna winced at the cynical twist of his mouth.

"I know you don't like people to think that, but I did. I really did," she said. "You see, it simply never occurred to me that you might be anything else other than Russian."

Count Czarski made no comment. He turned sharply away from her once more and seemed to stare out at the empty thoroughfare beneath the window.

As he did so, Roseanna observed that the paint on the window ledge where his fingers had been had begun to crumble under the pressure of his grip. And now that his hands were at his side, she saw that they were clenched so tightly that his knuckles were the color of parchment.

Roseanna's heart contracted fearfully as she went on:

"But when you . . . told us why you fought . . . against the Czar," she murmured, "I . . . I understood what you must have gone through. I . . . I believed you had done the right thing. I . . . I would have done the same . . . in your place."

She waited for him to speak, but there was no response—not even a hint that he had heard her.

"Oh, Marek!" she begged. "Please don't be cross with me!"

A long, shuddering sigh escaped the count. He wheeled round and took a step toward her. Then, very slowly and deliberately, he took a second step toward her.

Roseanna could not meet his glittering eyes. She looked down at her hands and trembled apprehensively as he strode across the carpet in her direction. Her heart pounded alarmingly as she sensed him coming nearer to her. She could see his hands, no longer clenched, but poised tensely at his side. He was in front of her now, not more than a foot from her. Timidly she put her own dainty hand forward and touched his.

Instantly he drew away from her.

Roseanna could scarcely control the sob in her throat. Instinctively she understood the reason for his action. He was afraid of permitting her to caress him—afraid of revealing his feelings—afraid of being hurt.

"And I can do nothing!"

She had to remain where she was, while he prowled around her in an ever-widening circle. He went farther and farther from her until he was in the shadows behind her.

Roseanna turned her head.

"How dark the interior of the sitting room is!" she reflected.

It seemed much gloomier than she remembered it. So very dark. She could hardly see Count Czarski, much less read his expression any more. But she realized that he was about to speak and she held her breath.

"Everything depends on what he says now!" she told herself.

10

"Why have you come?" Count Czarski demanded, in a voice she scarcely recognized. "To tell me that you were compelled to write that letter?"

Roseanna guessed what he had left unsaid. If it were merely that, she could easily have asked Denis to explain things to him. If it were merely that, then there was no need for the embarrassment of this confrontation between them.

"N-n-not entirely," she stammered.

"Not entirely?" he repeated blankly.

Roseanna found herself staring at her own feet. She was wearing orange slippers with dark brown embroidery, which matched her flame-colored gown. It was her favorite attire. Did he like it too? She hoped so. She had put it on specially for him.

"Mama may have meant what was in that letter," she stated. "I certainly did not." There was a slight pause and then she queried.

"Did you mean the reply?"

"I answered as I believed I had to ... in the circum-stances," he said. "Naturally if you ... if you wish me to go out of your life ... I shall do so."

As Roseanna heard his words, it seemed as if her heart turned to stone.

"I have never forced my presence on any woman," he concluded.

Roseanna felt she would die of misery.

"If Mama and Mr. Sandford had not been there," she responded in a low voice, "I should never have written that wretched note."

"Really?" Count Czarski questioned.

"He doesn't believe me!" she thought.

That hurt. The agony was almost unbearable. And then, quite suddenly, Roseanna was very angry. How dared he doubt her!

"*I'm* not the one who had you investigated!" she snapped at him. "*I* never wanted to start accusing you of anything!"

"But you were shocked by what was uncovered," Count Czarski returned.

"Surprised," Roseanna corrected.

For a split second their eyes met. But Roseanna was unable to bear his gaze and she glanced downward once more.

"You never asked me about my past," he remarked.

"It never occurred to me to do so," she told him.

"Why not?"

"Because it didn't matter."

"What!" he exclaimed.

"It didn't matter," Roseanna reiterated. "It was over and done with before we were introduced to one an-other, so it was no longer important. And Denis seemed to think well of you. You were friends, and ..."

She stopped speaking and shrugged.

"What are you trying to tell me?" Count Czarski inquired. "That you trusted me? That you accepted me as I was?"

"Yes," Roseanna answered truthfully.

In an instant he had crossed the space between them to her side and his arms went around her. Roseanna

97

gave a tiny cry and clung to him. She felt him brush away the tears that had come unbidden to her eyes. Then his lips were on hers, burning like fire.

Presently he released her.

"Roseanna, I love you," he murmured.

It was then that a sigh of relief escaped from her.

"I love you too, Marek," she whispered.

His arms tightened again. He was holding her so close that she could hardly breathe. She wondered vaguely whether she would be crushed to death in his embrace. Then his grip relaxed and he looked down at her. His eyes were smiling, yet anxious.

"Do you love me enough to come to America with me?" he questioned.

Roseanna stared at him. "So you were serious!" she cried. "You didn't say that to . . . to . . ."

To get at her. To wound her. To hurt her so much that she cried until she had no more tears left to shed.

"I am serious," he stated before she could complete her sentence.

"But why?" she wanted to know.

"Don't you see?" he queried. "I cannot stay in England. Oh, I am half English, so I suppose my own relations would accept me, but . . ."

"You are half English?" Roseanna asked in amazement.

"Yes," he confirmed. "My mother was English."

Roseanna's face clouded.

"What is it?" he inquired.

"Denis told me that your mother . . . was sent to Siberia by the Czar," she replied.

All at once a bitter expression swept across his face. Roseanna had never seen so much unhappiness. A thousand wounds with salt poured in them could not convey the amount of pain . . .

"It was due to her being English," he explained. "We—friends of ours and other members of the family—tried to warn her that she would be regarded as an enemy alien, because Russia and England were at war at the time, but she would not listen. She wanted desperately to try to save my father and my brother..."

Then his voice trailed away into nothing.

Roseanna drew his head down so that she could kiss him. When she looked at him again, there was no trace of the agony she had just witnessed.

"But you never said you were... half English... when you came to call," she pointed out.

"I did not intend to let anyone know," Count Czarski responded.

"Why not?"

"Why should your precious Mr. Sandford know, eh? Why should anyone know besides ourselves?"

Roseanna had no answer for that. The fact of his Englishness, like the fact of his Polishness, was unimportant: Marek was still Marek, wheresoever his parents or his grandparents had been born. And that was the only thing that mattered.

"Besides," Count Czarski continued, "the Polish side of me gets the uppermost nearly all the time."

"What do you mean?" Roseanna asked.

"Haven't you noticed?" he teased. "I am hot-blooded, quarrelsome, impatient, touchy, bad-tempered, uncivilized, and... passionate."

He glanced at her to see what impact his words had had. But there was no indication of anything, apart from a tiny worried little frown, as though she were aware that she had missed their significance.

"Hmmmmm," Roseanna mused. "So that is why you speak English so well."

Count Czarski nodded in assent. "Yes," he confirmed. "Since my mother was English, we children learned that language from her."

"Oh. And are you really going to go to America?"

"Yes."

"But why?"

Count Czarski drew a deep breath.

"I cannot return to Poland. If I did, I would undoubtedly be executed for treason, since I waged war against the Czar." He bit his lip. "I have been too much Napoleon's ally and campaigned too hard for my country's freedom. Now it is impossible for me to go back there.

I have to emigrate, to make a new life for myself. And America seems like a good place for that."

"Why don't you stay here?" Roseanna inquired. "Then perhaps one day..."

He laid his finger on her lips, silencing her before she could complete her suggestion.

"No," he replied. "It would be unrealistic."

"But Poland won't remain under Russian rule forever. One day it may be freed and—"

"Not in our lifetime," he interrupted.

"But—"

"No buts," he countered. "When I fought alongside the French army, independence was a dream that might have come true. Now it is nothing more than an illusion."

"Why?"

"Because everyone is tired of war. Europe is tired. Russia is tired. Poland is tired," he explained. "And when my people are ready to do battle once more, we shall either be too old to join in...or dead and buried and forgotten."

Roseanna was saddened by his words. And because she understood how much his country meant to him, she asked:

"Couldn't you get a pardon from the Czar?"

Count Czarski shrugged. "It is unlikely," he replied, "but even if it were possible, I would not want to go back now."

"Why not?"

"I could not stand idly by and watch as my people were dragged down into slavery," he told her. "No. No. I shall go to America and start a new life there. But will you come with me?"

Roseanna hesitated.

"What is it?" he questioned.

"I...I...can't really see myself as a frontiers-woman," she prevaricated.

"Who ever said anything about the frontier?"

"Well...America. You know."

"No. I don't. Please explain."

"Er...um...well...I mean...I can't sew skins

"...and I don't know what berries are edible and what aren't," Roseanna enumerated uneasily. "And I can't cook over a log fire.... And I don't think I could learn any of the red Indian languages. They seem so very different from English. Besides, I'm used to running a household with servants...and I couldn't manage on my own...and I don't know how to walk on snowshoes. And I can't...Why are you laughing?"

Count Czarski, who had been listening wide-eyed with wonderment to Roseanna's impression of the United States, finally could not contain his mirth any longer. Hearing him made Roseanna's heart bound with joy. He had a beautiful, musical, rich laugh, full of good humor and mischief.

"You speak as if you believe America is a kind of primitive wilderness," he responded, "a cross between the Yorkshire moors and the North Pole on an inclement November morning, where the people are clad in animal skins, live out in the open, and feed themselves on a meager diet of foliage, roots, and berries."

Roseanne pouted.

"Do you think that?" he demanded.

"Yes."

"Well, it isn't."

"Isn't it?" Roseanna countered stubbornly. "Hah!"

"There are cities there as well, with homes and shops and carriages. They even have paved streets, just like London."

"How do you know?"

"I sent my sister, Katarzyna, and my brothers Jerzy and Zdzislaw over some years ago. They live there now."

"Oh."

"Katarzyna writes long, entertaining letters about the American way of life," he explained. "Jerzy and Zdzislaw do too, but they are not as good correspondents as Katarzyna."

"Oh. What cities have they told you about?"

"The ones they have lived in," he said casually. "New York, Boston, Philadelphia, and Washington."

"They seem to have a rather nomadic existence."

"They are adventurous," he allowed. "Far more so than you."

"What do you mean?" Roseanna asked indignantly.

"I would guess you've never been out of London in your entire life."

"I have too!" Roseanna defended. "I've been to Nottingham and I've been to Brighton!"

Count Czarski, who had traveled thousands of miles across Europe, hooted with laughter.

"There you are, you see," he stated. "The exception proves the rule."

Roseanna was tongue-tied. She grimaced and he kissed her lips, leaving her tingling all over.

"America is full of sizable towns that have been built up over the last hundred years," Count Czarski informed her.

"Did your sister and brothers tell you that?" Roseanna wondered.

Count Czarski smiled curiously. "I have been learning about my new country," he answered.

"Oh."

"Don't you think one should study a place before one decides whether or not one is going to spend the rest of one's life there?"

"I suppose so." Pause. "Where in America did you intend to settle?"

"I shall probably build a house in Philadelphia," he said.

"Why?"

"Katarzyna is married to an American, a native of that town," he explained. "Jerzy and Zdzislaw plan to settle there too."

"Oh."

"It's one of the older towns I told you of, founded more than a hundred and thirty years ago," he remarked. "I believe it has one of two brick houses and even the odd servant."

Roseanna, realizing the he was making fun of her, bridled.

"Marek!" she began. "You—"

Her response was drowned in a sea of kisses. Then

102

he smiled at her with that charming smile of his that made her heart turn over and over and over.

Roseanna felt her resistance weakening.

"But," she protested, "it is very *wild* in America, isn't it?"

"What do you mean?"

"There are a lot of forests and mountains, and miles and miles of wilderness between the cities. Aren't there?" she inquired. "And big bears? And wolves?"

"Yes."

Roseanna shuddered.

"Roseanna, do you believe that Europe is totally devoid of these things?" Count Czarski questioned.

"Isn't it?"

"Of course not. There are the steppes of Russia, the Alps, the Pyrenees, the highlands of Scotland. We have wolves and bears, not to mention highwaymen, smugglers, and other undesirables." He paused and regarded her impishly. "I believe there are even some forests and a few tiny hills in England. And some of the towns are actually more than five miles apart. Of course they are nowhere near London or Nottingham or Brighton, but I have it on good authority—"

"Oh, you are horrible to tease me!" Roseanna cried, stamping her foot.

"It is you who are teasing me," he retorted.

Roseanna frowned, not comprehending.

"Will you come?" he persisted. "Or not?"

11

"Yes, I'll come," Roseanna answered.

She was glad that she had agreed to emigrate with him. He was so happy when she said "yes." She had never known a man to show his pleasure like that. He showered her with kisses, and when he released her, she was breathless ... and quite disheveled.

"I shall have to tidy myself up before I go home," she stated as she caught a glimpse of herself in the mirror over the fireplace.

Count Czarski consulted his watch.

"You will return to North Row in time for lunch?" he asked.

"Yes."

"What will you tell your family?"

"About this?"

"Yes."

"Nothing."

"Nothing!" Count Czarski exclaimed. "But what will

happen when your mother wants to know where you have been?"

"Oh, we've taken care of that."

"We?"

"Denis, Evelina, and I," Roseanna clarified. "We've decided what we are going to say—"

"—and it won't be anything about coming to see me," Count Czarski concluded.

"Definitely not. That will be a secret between Denis and Evelina and ourselves."

"I see. And what are you going to tell your mother, then?"

"When we meet, before we go to North Row, Evelina will tell me everything she and Denis did together this morning," Roseanna responded. "I shall learn as much as I can about Mr. Town's paintings on velvet and *The Battle of Vitoria* so that Mama will never suspect what I have really been doing."

"Hmmmmm," Count Czarski murmured. "And whose idea was this? Yours?"

"Partly. And Denis's."

"What has Denis got to do with this?"

Roseanna sighed. "We... Denis and I... believe Mama is trying to make us marry," she explained. "We're fond of each other, but neither of us wants that, so when Denis knew that you and I..."

"Ah, yes, I understand," Count Czarski commented.

"Anyway, Denis and I are *not* going to be seen anywhere on our own any more," Roseanna concluded firmly.

"No, of course not."

Count Czarski comprehended perfectly. If Mrs. Poulet wished the cousins to wed, then she might conceivably have mentioned the possibility to her neighbors.

It would not take long for a rumor to start and for people to consider that Denis Martin and Roseanna were together a great deal. Gossip was dangerous. Whispers could soon become ugly, damaging slanders. Then Denis and Roseanna might be forced to marry in order to keep their good names.

Roseanna redid her hair and put on her bonnet. As Count Czarski draped her cloak over her shoulders, she frowned as if puzzled. He put his hand under her chin and tilted her head up so that she looked into his eyes.

"You want to know when you will see me again?" he asked softly.

"Yes," Roseanna answered.

"Soon," he promised her tenderly. "Very soon."

Denis Martin's carriage was waiting for her as he had assured her it would be, and he helped her to ascend.

"Well?" Evelina demanded as Roseanna took her place beside her. "How did it go?"

"It's all right," Roseanna replied. "We have made up."

"Thank heavens for that!" Denis exclaimed with feeling.

Roseanna laughed. "I'm so glad you approve, Denis," she said. "Now, Evelina, you must tell me everything that you two did this morning."

"Where shall I begin?" Evelina countered.

"Did you enjoy it?" Roseanna questioned.

"Yes, I did. Very much. It was absolutely marvelous!" Evelina cried enthusiastically.

"I'm delighted to hear it," Denis commented wryly.

Roseanna and Evelina laughed.

"You keep out of this!" Evelina admonished, wagging her finger at him.

"Shan't!" Denis contradicted with mock petulance.

"Please don't interrupt, Denis," Roseanna urged. "Remember, this is serious. I have to memorize every single detail. Go on, Evelina! Tell me what happened!"

Evelina launched into a glowing account of the panorama of *The Battle of Vitoria*. She then went on to describe Mr. Town's shop where the paintings on velvet were displayed.

Roseanna had never listened so attentively to anything in her life. She learned as much as she could so that she would be able to reply to her mother's interrogation when they reached North Row.

"Did you enjoy yourselves?" was the first thing Mrs. Poulet wanted to know.

Roseanna, thinking of Count Czarski, blushed.

"Yes," she responded truthfully. "Very much."

"We had a marvelous time, Aunt," Evelina added. "Thank you for allowing us to go."

"Yes, thank you," Denis stated. "We spent an extremely pleasant morning together."

"I'm glad to hear it," Mrs. Poulet returned. "Will you be staying for lunch, Denis?"

"Er—I'm sorry, Aunt, but I can't," said Denis.

"Oh, what a pity!" Evelina exclaimed.

"Yes, it is a shame," Roseanna concurred.

"We're having your favorite, squab pie," Mrs. Poulet remarked.

The thought of lamb chops with apples and sugar done in one of Mrs. Poulet's light pastry cases was very tempting.

"Sounds absolutely delicious," Denis Martin murmured hungrily. "But . . . no."

"Are you sure you can't stay, Denis?" Mrs. Poulet persisted. "We would love to have you, you know that."

"Yes Aunt, but . . . well, I have an engagement . . . a business engagement," Denis prevaricated. "It will be dreadfully tedious, but I am having luncheon with a business acquaintance. It's the only time we have been able to set aside . . . to discuss—er—business."

"Oh. I see," Mrs. Poulet said, slightly bewildered by his manner. "Well, I suppose it can't be helped. Perhaps next time."

"Yes," Denis responded. "I'll be happy to come another time."

"Do that," Mrs. Poulet stated.

"Thank you," Denis concluded. "I'm afraid I've got to dash. Good-bye."

"Good-bye, Denis."

The others only just managed to call out to him as he raced down the garden path to where his carriage was waiting.

Mrs. Poulet smiled as Roseanna and Evelina recounted the events of the morning to her during lunch. She believed that the affair between Denis Martin and Roseanna was progressing satisfactorily. She was naturally disappointed that he had not proposed to her daughter. However, she was certain that since, in her opinion, Roseanna had now recovered from her unfortunate infatuation with Count Czarski, and since the way was no longer blocked by the man, she would accept her cousin's offer of marriage when he made it.

After lunch, when the cousins were alone in Roseanna's room, Evelina spoke.

"I'm glad I agreed to help you out," she remarked.

"Are you?" Roseanna queried.

"Yes. Now."

"Weren't you before?"

"I had my doubts about the wisdom of it," Evelina replied. "But I can see it was the right thing to do."

"How?"

"From your appearance."

"Am I different in some way?"

Evelina nodded in assent. "I cannot tell you how much better you look today than you did yesterday," she informed her.

"I was never happy about sending that terrible letter to Marek," Roseanna confessed.

"I realize that."

"I love Marek," Roseanna told her cousin. "I hope we'll be married soon."

Evelina started. "Is it wise to think like that, Roseanna?" she questioned.

"Of course. Why do you ask?"

"Marek fought against us during the war. He may be anti-English, and..."

Roseanna shook her head in negation. "No, no, Evelina," she corrected gently. "Marek didn't fight *against* England, but *for* Poland."

Evelina drew a deep breath. "Well!" she exclaimed. "That's one problem *I* wouldn't like to have to sort out!"

Roseanna smiled, then frowned.

"Naturally we shall have difficulties," she admitted, "particularly in winning over Mama..."

"I'll say!" Evelina declared. "You'll have to be *very* patient there!"

Yes. They would. It could take years, unless...

"If only Denis were to announce his intention of marrying someone else!" Roseanna cried.

"What do you mean?" Evelina queried.

"If he were to become engaged to another lady," Roseanna explained, "he could hardly be expected to propose to me. Then, once Mama understands that there was never anything between us, she might come round to the idea of my marrying Marek."

"Hmmmmm."

"You don't agree?"

"Oh, yes. It's not that."

"What then?"

"You weren't thinking of speeding up the process, were you?"

"Pardon?"

"You're not contemplating finding someone for Denis and pushing him into marriage with her, are you?"

"Heavens no. I wouldn't do anything so unkind. I simply wish that he had found someone. It would make life easier."

"Yes. It would. Br-r-r-r!" Evelina shivered.

"Cold?"

"Yes, I am. Excuse me a minute. I'm going to get my wrap."

Evelina ran out of Roseanna's room at the rear of the house and across the hallway to her own, which was at the front. Seconds later she rushed back into her cousin's chamber.

"Roseanna!" she whispered hoarsely.

Roseanna stared at Evelina's face, which had drained of color.

"What's the matter?" she asked.

"Marek!" Evelina hissed. "He is here!"

Roseanna jumped up with a start.

"What!" she exclaimed. "Marek? Here?"

"Yes. He is at the door. Now!"

Roseanna's own countenance turned ashen.

"No!" she gasped. "It's not possible!"

She dashed out of her room into her cousin's and gazed out of the window.

Evelina had been right. Count Czarski was outside, knocking on the door. It was being opened. He was admitted. In a couple of seconds he would be shown into the drawing room, where Mrs. Poulet was resting after her midday meal!

"You said nothing about this to me," Evelina accused softly.

"I knew nothing about it," Roseanna answered in a low voice.

"You saw Marek this morning. Surely—"

"No," Roseanna interrupted. "He did not mention that he was going to come here today."

Evelina sucked in her breath.

"Someone is going to be in for it!" she declared darkly.

Roseanna closed her eyes in despair. Evelina was right, of course. And the person *in for it* would, most likely, be her.

"Oh, no!" she groaned.

She had fondly imagined Count Czarski being prepared to wait patiently until she decided to risk breaking the news to her mother that they were still seeing each other. Naturally that meant delaying things for a while, but surely it was worth keeping their reconciliation a secret in order to let Mrs. Poulet get used to the idea—and to recover from the shock of learning that she and Denis were *not* going to get married.

Step by step, so Roseanna had hoped, they could have worked to bring Mrs. Poulet round, and then . . .

"Oh, Marek!" she wondered silently. "Why didn't you tell me you wanted to come and see Mama today?"

She could almost hear him answer her:

" . . . *the Polish side of me gets the uppermost nearly all the time . . . I am hot-blooded, quarrelsome, impatient . . .*"

Roseanna gnawed her lip. "If he sees Mama now, there is no telling what might happen!" she thought.

Why hadn't he given her any inkling of his intentions? Why . . . ?

Suddenly she froze as it dawned on her that he had intimated this when they parted:

"You want to know when you will see me again?"
"Yes."
"Soon," he had promised her. *"Very soon."*
Roseanna closed her eyes in agony. The word seemed to reverberate around her.
Soon. Soon. Soon. Soon. Soon....

12

Count Czarski was ushered into Mrs. Poulet's drawing room.

The latter was stunned to see him. Until now she had been under the impression that the letter she had compelled Roseanna to write, coupled with his distant though polite reply, meant that he would never set foot in the house in North Row again. It was a shock to discover that she had been mistaken.

"I apologize for disturbing you, madam," Count Czarski stated, "but I would like to speak to you in private."

Mrs. Poulet, still in a daze, nodded slightly, indicating that the maid who had admitted the count might leave them.

As the door closed behind the servant, Mrs. Poulet faced her visitor squarely.

"What is it?" she demanded in hostile tones.

"I have come to ask for your daughter Roseanna's hand in marriage," Count Czarski informed her bluntly.

Mrs. Poulet gasped in horror. "What!" she exclaimed.

Count Czarski repeated his request.

Mrs. Poulet stared at him in disbelief for a few seconds. Then, suddenly, she found her voice.

"Never!" she screamed at him. "Never! Never! Never! Never! Get out of my house! Get out at once! Never! Never! Never! You shall never marry Roseanna! Never while I live! Do you hear me?"

"Perfectly," Count Czarski returned.

He bowed, mockingly, infuriating Mrs. Poulet even more. Then he departed.

Meanwhile, from her vantage point on the stairs, where she and Evelina had gone to try to learn what was happening, Roseanna saw Count Czarski leave. When she saw how set his face was, her heart contracted. What had made him look so angry? What had her mother said?

"Marek!" she called out.

But it was too late. Count Czarski had already shut the front door behind him and Roseanna's strangled cry was lost in the sound of it slamming.

Evelina ran downstairs to the drawing room, dragging an unwilling Roseanna after her. They found Mrs. Poulet still sitting in the chair where she had been when Count Czarski had entered, a picture of indignation and fury.

"What has happened, Aunt?" Evelina inquired.

But Mrs. Poulet was too angry to respond. She tried to speak but she could only splutter with rage.

Just then there was a knock at the door. Roseanna and Evelina glanced at each other. Surely it could not be Count Czarski returning?

Seconds later, the maid admitted Mr. Sandford.

"I saw Lord Czarski leaving," he commented as he entered the drawing room. "Did he come here to see you?"

"Yes, he did!" Mrs. Poulet exclaimed, her tongue suddenly loosened.

"What ever did he want?" Mr. Sandford wondered.

"He asked for Roseanna's hand in marriage!" Mrs. Poulet declared.

"No!" Mr. Sandford cried. "What an outrageous thing to do! The fellow is a scoundrel!"

"I agree," Mrs. Poulet stated. "It was monstrous of him. He should never even have contemplated it!"

"Quite so," Mr. Sandford said.

"Why not?" Roseanna queried.

"Pardon?" Mr. Sandford questioned.

"Why shouldn't Marek have asked for my hand in marriage?" Roseanna wanted to know.

"Why not? Why shouldn't—?" Mrs. Poulet began to repeat. "Didn't you hear him when he was here before? Didn't he admit to being a prisoner of war and an enemy of our country? Didn't you listen when he told us he is Polish?"

"I can't see anything wrong with that," Roseanna defended.

Mrs. Poulet looked as if she were about to pass out.

"Smelling salts!" Mr. Sandford ordered.

Evelina reached into her reticule for some and handed them to Mr. Sandford, who, with his arms around the half-fainting widow, administered them.

"Oh!" Mrs. Poulet gasped, as she recovered. "That a daughter of mine . . . ! That I should ever live to see the day . . . ! Oh, my innocent little girl! He has seduced her! He has destroyed her good name!"

Roseanna flushed. "Marek has done nothing of the kind, Mama," she returned.

"Hah!" Mrs. Poulet exclaimed. "That kind of man has been the ruin of many a pretty young girl. And when the neighbors hear of this visit, you'll rue the day you ever set eyes on him!"

Roseanna frowned. She had been brought up to believe that it was a good sign when a man asked for your hand in marriage—not the reverse.

"You are being unreasonable," she insisted.

"*I* am being unreasonable!" Mrs. Poulet echoed. "The insolence of it! This . . . this child, Mr. Sandford . . . this baby . . . this infant here! Listen how she dares to answer back to her mother! I would never have dreamt of speaking to *my* mama like that! Ooh-ooh-ooh! It is insupportable!"

"You are right," Mr. Sandford concurred. "You are absolutely right, Mrs. Poulet. It is disgraceful!"

"I knew *you* would understand, Mr. Sandford," Mrs. Poulet purred. "Can you imagine how I felt when that . . . that wretch sought my permission for them to marry?"

"I can indeed. But you need not worry," Mr. Sandford assured her. "There is no question of Roseanna wedding that savage. Calm yourself, madam. I beg you. They shall not be joined together while I can prevent it. I swear it!"

Roseanna went cold. She glanced at Evelina and saw that her cousin's face was as white as she knew her own must be.

How could Mr. Sandford make a promise like that! He was not related to Roseanna! Legally he had no say in the matter whatsoever! The arrogance! The effrontery of it!

Meanwhile, Mrs. Poulet allowed herself to be comforted by Mr. Sandford's words and made an effort to pull herself together.

"Your daughter has been cruelly deluded by that wicked man," Mr. Sanford told her.

This was too much for Roseanna.

"Marek is not wicked!" she cried indignantly. "And he has not deluded me! It is you who are iniquitous, interfering where you have no business to and telling lies about Marek!"

Evelina stifled a gasp of surprise. She had never heard Roseanna talk like that to anyone. She longed to add something of her own, but she knew that it was wiser to remain quiet.

"I am only a poor relation," she reminded herself as she retained her self-imposed silence with considerable difficulty. "At the moment everyone is so agitated that if I utter a single word I shall land myself in serious trouble."

It wasn't easy for Evelina to keep her mouth shut.

Roseanna was like a sister to her, and it upset her to see her suffer.

"But what else can I do?" she reflected. "If I side with Roseanna it won't make things any better. Oh, that wretched Mr. Sandford. It is all his fault. Roseanna is quite correct. He ought not to have meddled. Stupid, interfering, pompous busybody! Who does he think he is?"

Evelina was thankful that no one had mentioned Roseanna's trip to the Albany that morning to see Count Czarski. If that had come out, there really would be weeping and wailing and gnashing of teeth!

At the height of the argument, the door opened and Denis Martin walked in unannounced, as was his wont. Mrs. Poulet gave an anguished cry, leaped up from her chair, flung herself into his arms, and burst into tears.

Poor Denis did not know what had hit him. He was slightly embarrassed by his aunt's display of emotion and he endeavoured to calm her. Gently he disentangled her from himself and led her to the sofa, where she seated herself.

"What has happened?" Denis Martin inquired solicitously, when it seemed as though Mrs. Poulet might be able to answer him. "Why are you so upset?"

"That . . . that odious Lord Czarski has just called!" Mrs. Poulet informed him.

Denis Martin frowned. "Why?" he wanted to know.

"To ask for Roseanna's hand in marriage!" Mrs. Poulet replied.

Denis was surprised but not unduly concerned.

"And did you consent?" he questioned.

Mr. Sandford was appalled.

"Consent!" he exclaimed in shocked tones. "She did no such thing! She refused him, of course!"

"There is no *of course* about it," Denis retorted.

"You don't seriously think I should have considered Lord Czarski's request, do you?" Mrs. Poulet queried.

"Yes, I do."

"Really, Denis!"

"You certainly ought not to have dismissed it so contemptuously," Denis Martin told her.

"Come, come now, sir..." Mr. Sandford began nervously.

"Why shouldn't you regard Marek as a suitor for Roseanna?" Denis Martin continued, ignoring Mr. Sandford. "He is wealthy, cultured, and titled—"

"Denis, how can you?" Mrs. Poulet interrupted. "Surely *you* understand why Lord Czarski is unsuitable?"

"I'm afraid I don't," Denis responded. "In my opinion, you ought to have evaluated his request as you would have done had it been any other nobleman."

"Denis!" Mrs. Poulet cried. "It is commendable to be fair, but this is carrying things too far!"

"I don't know what you mean," Denis Martin protested.

"You, of all people," Mrs. Poulet stated, "who have been courting my darling Roseanna these past few months—"

"I have been *what?*"

"Courting me," Roseanna told him.

Denis whirled round to face her. "You know very well that I have not been courting you!" he declared.

Roseanna nodded in assent. "Yes, Denis," she concurred.

Denis Martin rounded on Mrs. Poulet.

"Roseanna and I are not interested in marrying each other, Aunt," he informed her. "We would never have agreed to do so. Not in a thousand years. Is that not true, Roseanna?"

"Yes, it is," Roseanna answered. "And it has nothing to do with Marek. We would have felt this way whether he had come along or not."

"Exactly," Denis agreed.

At these words, Mrs. Poulet burst into tears once more.

Mr. Sandford seated himself on the sofa beside her and gave her his handkerchief.

"You have been deceiving your poor aunt, sir!" he accused Denis.

"She has been deceiving herself and you have been helping her to do so," Denis Martin contradicted. "I am sorry for it, but I stick to what I said earlier: You should not have dismissed Marek's offer for Roseanna's hand."

Mrs. Poulet, still weeping, raised her head and looked directly at her nephew.

"I cannot take any more," she sobbed. "I really cannot take any more."

"I am sorry if I have upset you, Aunt," Denis apologized, "but I believe it is time the truth was told. I do not love Roseanna. I never have been in love with her and I never could be in love with her. I am fond of her. She is a dear girl, but a romance between us is out of the question."

"Denis," Mrs. Poulet wept, "I must ask you to leave."

"Certainly, Aunt," Denis Martin replied, bowing. "Good day to you."

After the door had closed behind Denis Martin, an awkward silence fell in the room. Evelina and Mr. Sandford did not know what to say or do. Mrs. Poulet was still crying. Roseanna watched her for a few moments and then decided that she could not bear it. She came to her mother and sat down on her other side, hoping that she could perhaps make her see that it wasn't that bad.

"Get away from me!" Mrs. Poulet exclaimed as Roseanna touched her lightly.

Roseanna leaped to her feet as if she had been struck.

Mrs. Poulet's tears had suddenly vanished.

"Go upstairs!" she exclaimed angrily. "Go upstairs to the top room this instant!"

Roseanna was shattered. "What?" she asked, stunned. "What do you mean?"

"You treacherous, wicked, deceitful child!" Mrs. Poulet cried in strangled tones as she shook with rage. "I never thought I would live to hear a daughter of mine talk as impudently as you did before your cousin appeared!"

118

"I—" Roseanna began.

I was defending the man I love, a man whom you and Mr. Sandford between you were slandering mercilessly, for no good reason other than that you wanted me to marry someone else! she would have said.

But Mrs. Poulet was not listening.

"If Denis had not arrived at that moment," she went on, "I swear I would have lost my temper with you. Now will you do as I command you and go directly upstairs to the top room!"

Roseanna made no move to obey.

"Evelina!" Mrs. Poulet screamed hysterically. "Mr. Sandford! Be so good as to accompany us!"

"Mama—" Roseanna started.

"Be quiet, girl!" Mr. Sandford interrupted. "You have said enough! Can't you see how you have upset your poor dear mother?"

"I—" Roseanna tried to protest.

"And don't imagine you will be permitted to marry Lord Czarski," Mrs. Poulet continued, cutting her short, "whatever Denis said about considering his request! He is a monster and you were foolishly sinful to have encouraged him! But you will learn. Yes, my girl. You will discover what it is to bring your mother's wrath down upon yourself, Roseanna Poulet!"

"Wh-what do you m-mean?" Roseanna stammered.

"You'll see!" Mrs. Poulet promised, eyes flashing. "There will be no tea for you today and no supper tonight either!"

Roseanna stiffened. She knew that it was useless to argue. Mrs. Poulet was beside herself with fury, and reasoning with her was impossible. She could do nothing except follow her mother, who paused only to collect her daughter's nightdress on the way upstairs.

No one said a word throughout, but Roseanna found Evelina's comforting arm about her shoulders as they proceeded.

The uppermost room of the house was the billiard room, which Mr. Poulet had had built for himself. It was constructed in the form of a turret surrounded by windows on all sides so that it had the maximum amount of light, thus permitting him to enjoy his game for as long as possible.

The billiard room stood apart from the rest of the house. It was higher even than the attic where the servants slept. When her father had been alive, Roseanna had liked the place. She and Evelina had frequently gone up there to play. With squeals of delight they had endeavored to have a game of billiards, which, as young ladies, they were not supposed to do, but which an indulgent Mr. Poulet had allowed them to.

"It is different now, though," Roseanna reflected as she went up the steps.

A few months after Mr. Poulet's untimely death, the billiard table and the cues had gone. Mrs. Poulet had announced that the sight of them aggravated her grief, and in any case, since no one in the house other than her late lamented husband ever used them, it was pointless to keep them.

She had then remarked that the room would make a nice guest chamber for when Roseanna's brothers brought their friends home from boarding school for Christmas or Easter or for the summer holidays. And it had, accordingly, been refurnished for that purpose.

Tonight, though, Mrs. Poulet seemed to intend that it be turned into a prison.

"How could she?" Roseanna wondered.

She shivered apprehensively. There was something terrible about the prospect of being locked in this isolated room on her own. Her heart was in her mouth as they reached the landing outside it.

"I can't face it," she thought. "Perhaps if I ask Mama nicely, she'll let me stay in my own room instead."

Hurriedly she tried to frame the request in her mind before she uttered it.

Meanwhile, Mrs. Poulet took a key from the bunch that hung on a ring at her waist and unlocked the door.

"In!" she ordered peremptorily.

Roseanna gnawed her lip. It was no good to plead for leniency. As she stepped inside, she held her head high so that no one would guess how frightened she was.

120

Behind Mrs. Poulet, on the landing, stood Evelina and Mr. Sandford. The former looked worried. The latter gazed haughtily at Roseanna.

Mrs. Poulet handed her daughter her nightgown.

"When you have repented for the way you have behaved," she informed her, "when you are truly sorry for the disgusting exhibition you gave in front of your dear mama, then you may come downstairs again. Until then, however, you will remain confined up here."

Roseanna's mouth was dry. She had never seen her mother in this relentless, unforgiving mood before.

"Without food?" she queried anxiously.

Mrs. Poulet's face grew purple with rage.

"Are you endeavoring to make me out to be unjust, Roseanna?" she inquired evenly.

"No, Mama," Roseanna replied. "I was merely asking a question."

And a not unreasonable one in the circumstances.

Mrs. Poulet had already stipulated that her daughter was to be given no tea and no supper. Roseanna had thus had nothing to eat since lunch. She would be hungry soon. When would she be permitted food again? Tomorrow morning? Would she be allowed breakfast? Could she expect that or not?

"You will have no more food today," Mrs. Poulet reiterated, "as a punishment for your wickedness."

That was not a satisfactory answer as far as Roseanna was concerned.

"And ... tomorrow?" she persisted.

Mrs. Poulet eyed her coldly. "We shall see tomorrow whether your disposition is more amenable, my girl," she stated.

And with that she slammed the door on her daughter.

Roseanna shuddered as she heard the key turn in the lock. She knew that it was the only one to the room and that her mother would guard it closely, so that there was no chance of Evelina sneaking up with something for her to eat.

She backed away from the door and sank down onto

121

the bed, where she sat staring into space as she listened to the footsteps of the others receding into the distance.

Roseanna pictured their descent. Three steps downward would bring them from the landing outside the billard room to the attic corridor level, where there was another door to be opened and locked securely before one came to the servants' quarters.

"Mama has the key to that, too," Roseanna recollected. "Bother!"

If Evelina did intend to help her cousin out by bringing food to her, it made her task that much more difficult.

Roseanna grimaced. In her mind's eye she could see Mrs. Poulet, Mr. Sandford, and Evelina as they continued on their way to the ground floor. From the servants' quarters they would take the main staircase, which would bring them to the second floor of the house, where the family's bedrooms were, and ultimately to the ground floor, where they would probably repair to the drawing room.

"What will Mama do when they get there?" Roseanna wondered. "Serve tea, perhaps?"

It was the right time for it. And as she thought about it, she realized that she felt thirsty.

"I could do with a cup of tea now," she reflected wistfully, "or even a glass of water."

She looked around hopefully, but there was nothing either drinkable or eatable in the billiard room.

Roseanna made a face. She tried to imagine what Mrs. Poulet, Mr. Sandford, and Evelina would talk about. Her mother, she deduced, would undoubtedly go on and on and on about how miserable her "baby" had made her with her "disobedience."

"I am not a child any more, Mama!" Roseanna insisted. "I am not a child!"

And then she burst into tears.

13

After a while, Roseanna stopped crying and rose to her feet in order to examine the room where she was confined. Was there any chance of escaping? She rattled the doorknob to see if it would open, but that was useless. Then she glanced out of the window to try to find out if she could make her exit that way. But it was a l-o-o-o-ong way down. Knotting every single blanket and sheet together would not help her, especially since even looking down made her feel dizzy.

Roseanna came back to the center of the room and seated herself on the bed once more.

"It's so unfair!" she declared.

She was not accustomed to being treated so harshly. If she had been five years old and had indulged in a temper tantrum, perhaps she might have accepted it. If she had been deliberately rude or spiteful without cause, she might have allowed that her mother had some justification.

"But I am not five years old!" she thought indignantly. "And I wasn't the one who behaved badly, either!"

She was sixteen—not a child any more, but a young woman. And she had done nothing wrong. She had only defended the man she loved when he had been slandered.

Roseanna clenched her hands. She did not and never had wanted to marry Denis Martin. Her mother had imagined the whole affair between them. Thus her mother had no one except herself to blame that it had not worked out as she hoped.

"It certainly wasn't poor Marek's fault!" Roseanna cried. She let loose a shuddering sob. "I want to marry Marek and spend the rest of my life with him, and I have the right to make that decision!"

But alas! Even as she uttered the words, she knew that no one else would share her views.

As far as society was concerned, she was a child until she reached the age of twenty-one, and even then she was a woman who needed to be "protected." If her parents or her guardians chose not to allow her to marry the man she loved—for any cause whatsoever—then she had absolutely no right to question their wisdom. If she objected, she was wayward; if she obeyed but was miserable, she was being deliberately sulky.

Roseanna knew in her heart of hearts that if Mrs. Poulet disapproved of Count Czarski as her husband then society would side with her, and Roseanna herself would have no hope of being permitted to become his wife. Worse, her mother could force her to marry another man whom she felt was more suitable—provided one could be found.

Roseanna cringed at the idea.

"If Papa had been alive, none of this would ever have happened," she told herself.

It was not wishful thinking; it was true.

Mr. Poulet would have been worried about Count Czarski having fought for Napoleon, but he would have been prepared to listen to the count's point of view. And he would probably have accepted that Count Czarski could not have done otherwise.

Roseanna sighed. She knew that her father would

124

have discussed her future husband with her. He might have been upset at the notion of Roseanna marrying a foreigner and emigrating, but he would have understood. Furthermore, he would have given the couple his blessing as well as his consent.

"There is no reason why I should not marry Marek and go to America with him," Roseanna reflected. "It is not as though I am deserting Mama. Evelina will still be here to keep her company."

Besides, Roseanna had two brothers who would remain in England and who would look after Mrs. Poulet in her old age if she needed them to.

Roseanna sighed once more. If her father had been alive things would have been different.

"Papa would never have forced me to marry someone I didn't want," she mused, "nor have prevented me from becoming the wife of the man I loved."

Certainly if her father had been living her mother would not have been so beastly to Count Czarski.

Roseanna recalled her father's death only too clearly. Her childhood had come to an abrupt end then.

"Mama didn't understand," she thought.

Evelina was the only one who had comprehended what it meant. She had lost both her parents and therefore she knew what it was like.

"It made a difference for all of us—the boys too," Roseanna remembered.

It was not easy to say how her brothers had altered. But they were no longer as carefree as they had been earlier. They seemed suddenly to feel the burden of their responsibilities. They tried to grow up fast, to become men, so that they could take charge of things, even though they were younger than Roseanna herself.

"I suppose I must have changed in the same way," Roseanna reflected. "Yes, I did. Denis noticed. When he came back after he had been wounded, that first time when he met Marek, he said how much older I seemed."

Mrs. Poulet had believed that her nephew was

merely being kind. But he had meant it. Roseanna had become an adult that year . . . in many ways.

Roseanna recollected how she had told her brothers about their father's demise.

The boys had been home earlier that summer for a fortnight. Then they had gone to stay with some friends of theirs for a week. The day they had been due to return, their father had died.

Mrs. Poulet had been in too much of a state to see her sons. The shock of losing her husband so suddenly had overwhelmed her. She had been beside herself with grief. The doctor had prescribed a strong dose of laudanum and it had been left to Roseanna to break the news to her brothers.

"What do I say to them?" Roseanna had asked Evelina.

Evelina had shrugged. "There's not much you can say," she had answered. "Tell them the truth: that their father has had an accident and that he is dead."

"But that sounds so harsh," Roseanna had protested. "Isn't there any way I can . . ."

"Make it better?" Evelina had questioned bitterly. "Pretend he is only half dead?"

Roseanna had winced.

"Look," Evelina had explained, "when my parents died, certain people tried to convince me that they were still alive, but very ill. They held out the hope that they might recover . . . If I were a good girl, I—"

"But your parents were drowned at sea, weren't they?"

"Exactly. But they lied to me. They pretended they had been rescued and that they were seriously ill but that there might be a chance. It was several days before they told me the truth. Even though I suspected that something was wrong, even though I asked, they wouldn't tell me. They meant well. They wanted to give it to me in nice easy stages. But it was no good. Death is death. There is no way you can invent a euphemism for it, no way you can lessen the blow."

"All right," Roseanna had said unhappily. "I shall take your advice."

To her amazement, Roseanna had discovered that

Evelina was correct. She had told her brothers straight out, but even before she had uttered the words, her brothers had guessed that their beloved father was no more. And they had thanked her for telling them directly—"man to man"—instead of being precious and mealymouthed.

Roseanna sighed. Yes. That had been part of growing up. It had definitely left its mark on her. She had seen a new side of life. The happy childhood she had known was over; her adulthood had begun.

"I don't suppose Mama realized what a difference it made to me," Roseanna thought. "She wanted me to go on wearing pigtails and she would not let me put away my dolls."

Not, mind you, that Roseanna had been sorry to keep the dolls out, but neither she nor Evelina played with them any more.

Roseanna sighed again. "Mama behaves sometimes as though she believes I am still on leading strings!"

However, Mrs. Poulet could not keep the clock at the period when her daughter had barely begun to learn to walk. Time marched inexorably on. Roseanna and Evelina, as well as everyone they knew, were growing older.

"At least we got our coming-out party," Roseanna comforted herself.

But Mrs. Poulet had gone on and on and on about how young her daughter was and how she ought to wait until next year.

It was Denis Martin who had gently pointed out that Mrs. Poulet had married when *she* was sixteen, so it couldn't really be all that early for her daughter to come out.

"Was that when Mama decided that Denis and I should marry?" Roseanna wondered.

What a lot of trouble that idea had caused!

Roseanna grimaced as she recalled that terrible quarrel with her mother.

"Why did Mr. Sandford have to interfere? It was none of his business!" she thought. "I am not *his* daughter—thank heaven!"

Roseanna frowned. Denis Martin had been right to suspect that Mr. Sandford hoped to wed her mother.

"I don't mind Mama taking another husband, if only she lets me have the man I love . . . the only man I'll ever love," she added wistfully.

She tried to imagine what Count Czarski would do, now that he had been hurt and humiliated by Mrs. Poulet yet again.

"Will he be angry with me for that?" Roseanna asked. "Or not?"

How she wished she could talk to him!

Restlessly she stood up and went to the windows to look out once more. The drop to the ground seemed even greater than it had previously.

"Three floors!" Roseanna reflected. "Oh, no!"

It was impossible. The very notion made her shudder. Even so, she fingered the blankets tentatively as she endeavored to ascertain whether they would reach that far if they were tied together.

"It's no use," she decided.

They might be long enough, but she could neither guarantee that they would take her weight nor that any knot she made would hold until she was safely on the ground.

"I suppose I shall have to remain in here," she told herself.

Her tummy rumbled. She was hungry. She had not eaten much for lunch, she never did. She generally saved some room for tea with cake and scones. But she had missed that, thanks to the fight with her mother.

"They will probably have roast beef for dinner," Roseanna muttered, "and accompanying it . . ."

. . . Yorkshire pudding seething with the juice from the meat. Vegetables were scarce on account of the cold weather they had had that winter. Those that were available were expensive. But there would be roast potatoes and possibly some of the salted beans that her mother had done last summer, not to mention crisp pickled onions.

"What else will they have?" Roseanna wondered.

Sherry to start? Thick fish soup, maybe? And after

dinner a baked rice or vermicelli pudding, or perhaps a trifle made from macaroons left over from yesterday?

Roseanna could almost taste the repast.

"I must stop this!" she exhorted herself. "I shall go mad with hunger if I allow myself to dwell on food."

But how long would it be before her enraged mother permitted her to have any nourishment? Would she try to compel Roseanna to send another letter to Count Czarski saying that she would have nothing more to do with him? Would that be the price Roseanna would be expected to pay for her next meal?

"I'll never write anything like that again!" Roseanna exclaimed resolutely.

She could not bear the thought of seeing Count Czarski looking as he had done after he had received the last missive, the one her mother had composed.

"No! No! I couldn't do it! I couldn't! I couldn't!" Roseanna reiterated in an imaginary argument with Mrs. Poulet. "I would rather starve to death."

Roseanna paced up and down the room. Back and forth. Back and forth. She felt like a caged animal, and she walked around until she was giddy from doing so. Then she had another go at the door. But it was no good. It was too strong for her to break down. And the windows were too high for her to escape from.

"I never thought the billiard room would seem like a prison to me!" Roseanna reflected.

But unbelievably, that is what had happened. And she was as effectively confined in this former playroom as any unfortunate in the Tower of London.

"I don't suppose Mama will come back up to see me tonight," Roseanna mused. "Will she?"

She had a fleeting hope that Mrs. Poulet might relent and release her before daybreak. But a glance at the nightdress dashed it. Her mother had brought that up because she did not intend to return before morning.

Roseanna sighed for the umpteenth time.

"I shall have to go to bed," she decided.

But she was not the least bit tired and she was very, very hungry. She bit her lip.

"He who sleeps, eats," she tried to tell herself.

She returned to the bed and sat down on the edge of it, staring at the closed door as if she could mesmerize it into opening of its own accord.

It was no longer light out. The sun had set long ago, and it was growing darker with every passing second. Roseanna could hardly make out the gleaming lock in front of her.

"It must be about half past eight," she guessed.

The neighbors would be drawing their curtains soon, and the chandeliers would be lit. Outside in the street, the lamplighters were already beginning their rounds. And downstairs Mrs. Poulet and Evelina would probably be starting to have dinner.

"Will Mr. Sandford stay?" Roseanna wondered.

She could easily imagine him remaining to console Mrs. Poulet in her hour of desperate need.

Roseanna pictured the scene. Tea would have been later than usual on account of the upset, and that meant that dinner would be too.

Mrs. Poulet, Mr. Sandford, and Evelina would be seated in the dining room, which, since it overlooked the back garden, was out of sight of the hoi polloi who passed by the house either in hackney carriages or on foot.

Mrs. Poulet would take her usual place and would flatter Mr. Sandford by giving him Mr. Poulet's position at the head of the table. Evelina would sit in the middle and look askance, but make no comment, as Mrs. Poulet rambled on about how hard done by she was.

Roseanna's own place would be laid, but be pointedly empty: a grim reminder of the quarrel that had occurred.

When everyone was ready, grace would be said. Then the wine would be poured out and the servants would bring in a tureen of steaming hot, beautifully flavored soup....

"I really must stop thinking of food!" Roseanna told herself abruptly.

And that meant that she had to go to bed.

"Sleep will help me to forget! Remember," she urged herself, "everything looks better in the morning."

But though Roseanna knew her advice was sound, she did not make a move to undress. She was not so much sleepy as weary. A strange lassitude crept over her, robbing her of her energy.

"I wish I were dead!"

14

Meanwhile, earlier that day, unknown to Roseanna, Evelina had suddenly recalled after tea that she had forgotten to buy a pair of gloves.

"I shall have to go to Bond Street immediately to get them," she announced.

"Must you?" Mrs. Poulet inquired.

"Yes, Aunt," Evelina insisted. "The pair I have will never do for Lady Fane's on Saturday. And there won't be time tomorrow, so..."

"Oh, very well," Mrs. Poulet consented.

What Mrs. Poulet did not know was that Evelina's true purpose in going to Bond Street was that she hoped to be able to deliver a note she had secretly composed to Count Czarski.

As Evelina hurried toward the fashionable shopping area, she frowned, wondering how she was going to get her missive to the count without anyone discovering.

"If the maid finds out," Evelina thought, considering the presence of the servant trotting obediently behind her, "she will tell Aunt and there will be trouble. But how can I send word to Marek without her being aware of what I am up to?"

Then, as luck would have it, Evelina caught sight of Count Czarski's Polish manservant, Tomasz, who had been sent to Bond Street on a simple errand for his master.

Evelina's heart leaped. Without her maid noticing, she caught the old man's eye. Placing her fingers on her lips as a sign for him to be silent, Evelina bided her time.

Presently the right moment came. her maid was otherwise occupied and not watching her. Evelina was able to thrust the note into Tomasz's hand.

"For Lord Czarski!" she whispered urgently. "Hurry!"

Old Tomasz stared at her in astonishment, and for a second Evelina's heart stood still. Had he understood? He spoke only Polish. Perhaps he had failed to comprehend.

Then, to Evelina's relief, something, either her anxious tone, or Count Czarski's name, communicated itself to the man. He put the missive into his pocket and departed with all due speed for the Albany.

Evelina smiled and went on to make her purchase, a pair of lemon-colored gloves, before returning to North Row.

Roseanna heard a faint tapping on the windowpane. She ignored it. It came again. She ignored it again. It came yet again, irritating her and then finally rousing her from her reverie so that she looked to see what was causing it.

There was the count.

"I am dreaming," Roseanna reflected.

She pinched herself. Then she realized that she was fully awake, that Count Czarski really was outside her window, holding a lantern which was illuminated by a single candle, and that he was mouthing the words:

"Open up!"

Roseanna was galvanized into action. She ran toward him and undid the window latch.

Count Czarski leaned over the wooden sill and put his lantern down on the floor. Then he seated himself on the ledge, drew Roseanna close to him, and whispered soft, caressing endearments to her, half in Polish, which she did not understand, and half in English, which she did.

Roseanna had no idea how he had managed to come up to her, and she did not care. He was there. She could see him and touch him. That was enough. She was no longer alone. She was no longer frightened.

When Evelina came back from her shopping expedition, she found Mr. Sandford still at the house. Mrs. Poulet had invited him to stay for dinner, which he had persuaded her to delay until after eight, as the enormous tea they had consumed (both Mr. Sandford and Mrs. Poulet invariably ate more when they were angry) had taken away his appetite.

Eventually the three of them dined as Roseanna had imagined they would. The repast was excellent, and normally they would have been in high spirits on account of the superior quality of the food. But Mrs. Poulet felt uneasy. She had a mother's instincts, and she sensed that everything was not going as she had planned it.

As dinner progressed, Mrs. Poulet became more and more edgy. Then, when the meal had drawn to an end, she sent Evelina out of the room to fetch the cards so that the three of them could play whist.

While Evelina was gone, Mrs. Poulet turned to Mr. Sandford.

"I am beginning to wish that I had not locked Roseanna in that room," she remarked.

"You had no choice, madam," Mr. Sandford pointed out. "She was disobedient."

"Yes, but—"

"What else could you have done?"

"I don't know," Mrs. Poulet responded. "I am sure

it was the right thing, and yet I wish that I had not done it."

"But madam, discipline must be enforced."

"Yes."

"It is your duty as a mother to see that your children—your daughters particularly—are well bred."

In other words, meek, submissive, and servile.

"I agree with you," Mrs. Poulet stated, "but . . ."

Mr. Sandford took her hand in his and raised it to his lips.

"Your tenderness does you credit, madam," he said, "but you cannot allow yourself to surrender to it."

"No," Mrs. Poulet concurred. "You are correct."

Then she gave a long, despairing sigh.

"Madam, a night on her own is not such a harsh punishment for Roseanna," Mr. Sandford commented, "especially not after having upset you like that."

"I suppose not."

"And she can well do without dinner," Mr. Sandford added. "It will not do her any harm."

"So I have been telling myself."

"She can always make up for it tomorrow."

"Yes," Mrs. Poulet responded.

Still, her peace of mind was disturbed. Was it the nagging voice inside her making her aware that her late husband, Roseanna's father, would have handled the matter very differently? Or was it merely that she had a vague notion all was not well?

Before she could say any more, Evelina returned with the cards.

Mrs. Poulet made an effort to dismiss her uneasy thoughts. She observed that Mr. Sandford was in good spirits as he began to shuffle and deal. Evelina, too, seemed to have brightened up since this afternoon.

Mrs. Poulet ought to have been as cheerful as the other two. But, though whist was her favorite game, she did not enjoy playing it that evening. Despite having resolved to put Roseanna out of her mind, she was unable to do so.

"What is going on in the billiard room?" she wondered. "Should I have left Roseanna there on her own?"

Mrs. Poulet could not concentrate on the cards. She lost steadily, which was unusual for her. As time passed, her fears grew greater instead of diminishing, and when she heard the clock chime ten she started up out of her seat as nervously as a scalded cat.

"What ever is the matter, Aunt?" Evelina asked.

"Nothing," Mrs. Poulet answered.

"Then why are you so jumpy?" Evelina wanted to know. "Are you expecting someone?"

"No. No. It is nothing, I tell you!" Mrs. Poulet replied sharply.

Mr. Sandford frowned. He was not as insensitive to Mrs. Poulet's moods as he was to those of others around him. He guessed that Evelina was right. There was something wrong.

"What is it, my dear?" he queried.

Evelina's eyebrows arched as Mr. Sandford took her aunt's hand in his. Such familiarity!

"Well...we...I..." Mrs. Poulet began. "It is nothing I can put my finger on, but I feel uneasy about Roseanna being up there alone in that room."

"Perhaps we should go up and have a look at her," Mr. Sandford suggested, "just to reassure you."

"No!" Evelina exclaimed before she could stop herself. Hastily she covered her tracks. "She'll be asleep now, won't she? We'll only waken her!"

"Asleep?" Mrs. Poulet echoed. "Roseanna? At this hour?"

"Yes," Evelina reiterated. "Why not?"

"But Evelina, Roseanna is accustomed to staying up until after midnight," Mrs. Poulet protested, "particularly with those parties and trips to the theater you have been going on recently. And it is only ten o'clock now!"

"Is it?" Evelina asked innocently. "I thought it was later." She feigned a yawn. "I confess I am very tired."

"Didn't you count the chimes?" Mr. Sandford challenged.

"No," Evelina responded sweetly. "But then, I never do."

She yawned again, more convincingly.

"Oh, I see," Mr. Sandford muttered.

He didn't believe her, but as she had her back to the clock he was compelled to accept her word for it.

"I really am sleepy, Aunt," Evelina murmured. "I think I shall go directly to my room—if you two don't mind."

"Of course we don't mind," Mrs. Poulet returned.

"Not in the least," Mr. Sandford added.

Evelina started to rise. "I daresay Roseanna has gone to bed by now," she stated. "It would be a shame to waken her. Don't you agree, Aunt?"

"Hmmmm. Perhaps," Mrs. Poulet murmured.

"If Roseanna is asleep as you suggest," Mr. Sandford commented, "she would hardly hear her mother opening the door."

"You are right. Let's go up," Mrs. Poulet urged, "and have a look at her."

"Very well," Mr. Sandford concurred.

Evelina clicked her tongue in annoyance.

"I'll come with you," she said. "If Roseanna is awake, I can bid her good night. We usually do that, you know."

"Yes, do join us, Evelina," Mrs. Poulet stated.

"Thank you, Aunt," Evelina acknowledged.

And the three of them made their way out of the dining room, upstairs to the billiard room.

Suddenly, Roseanna remembered that she was still a prisoner.

"If Mama catches you up here, Marek, she'll be furious!" she declared.

"I sincerely hope she does not come up just yet," Count Czarski responded.

"You ... you have to ... go ... now."

Roseanna nearly choked as she uttered the words. Even the notion of sending him away was unbearable. But it had to be done—for his sake.

"I agree," Count Czarski answered. "Are you ready?"

"Ready?" Roseanna repeated. "For what?"

"To leave," he clarified.

"With ... you?"

"Of course."

Roseanna stared at him in astonishment.

137

"You didn't think I would go without taking you along with me, did you?" he demanded.

Roseanna swallowed. "I . . . I never . . . considered . . . that," she murmured.

She peered apprehensively out of the window. It was dark by then, so dark that she could see nothing beyond Count Czarski himself, save only the topmost part of a very long ladder, which he had used to reach her eyrie.

"Well, consider it now," he commanded.

"You . . . you mean . . . you want me to . . . run away with you?" Roseanna asked nervously.

It was not something a young lady in her position had been brought up to do. Newspapers of the day spoke of ladies who ran away from home in the same disparaging tones they reserved for murderers, thieves, and . . . fallen women!

Then there was the question of climbing down. She could hardly be expected to look forward to that prospect!

Count Czarski sensed that her hesitation was due more to her fear of the long descent than to her balking at the impropriety of departing from North Row in his company.

He smiled tenderly at her. "Don't worry," he said. "I won't let anything happen to you."

Roseanna eyed Count Czarski questioningly.

"I shall go down first," he explained. "If you do miss your footing, I shall be there to catch you."

"Oh," Roseanna responded. "Hmmmmm."

In a split second she reviewed the alternatives. She could refuse to go with Count Czarski, giving as her excuse the fact that she was a dutiful daughter. But what was in store for her if she remained? Would she be starved into submission by her mother? Would she be forced to reject Count Czarksi and compelled to marry a man she hated—or worse, to stay an old maid, embittered and lonely for the rest of her days?

Roseanna knew that convention demanded that she stay. Society regarded her predicament as being entirely her own fault. She had disobeyed her mother.

She should have done as she had been told to and cut Count Czarski out of her life.

"But if I do that," she reflected, "Mama is certain to make me swear never to wed Marek."

But how unfair that was!

"I might be only sixteen, but I know my own mind," she thought.

She had found the man who was right for her. Why should she wait endless long years in order to marry him? Why shouldn't she run away with him that very night?

"Yes, I'll come," Roseanna decided.

Count Czarski kissed her.

"But before we go," Roseanna continued, "It might be a good idea to fix the bed so that it looks as though I am asleep in it."

"Yes," Count Czarski agreed. "Let me help you."

"No! No!" Roseanna cried as he swung his leg over the window ledge and started to enter the room. "Stay where you are! I don't want anyone to hear you!"

Count Czarski remained in his place, sitting astride the window, with one foot inside the billiard room and the other foot dangling outside it.

Meanwhile, Roseanna picked up the lantern he had deposited on the floor earlier and put it beside the bed, which she began to rearrange. There was just sufficient light from the solitary candle in the lantern to enable her to see what she was doing.

The bed in the billiard room had been made up for winter. Two thick woolen blankets covered it; a top sheet and a bottom sheet lay beneath them.

Roseanna stripped the bed completely. She took the bottom blanket and rolled it up in a form which was about her size. Then she stuffed it inside her nightdress so that it would appear to be her. A couple of cushions from one of the chairs were put into the nightdress's sleeves to resemble her arms. The sheet made the form of her head.

When Roseanna was satisfied, she covered her makeshift effigy with the other sheet and blanket and tucked the bedclothes in. The chair, which she had robbed of its cushions, she disguised by draping the counterpane apparently haphazardly over it.

"There!" she announced as she finished. "What do you think?"

Count Czarski nodded in approval. "Excellent," he said.

The form in the bed looked exactly as he would have imagined Roseanna to appear when she was fast asleep. From a distance, especially in the dark, it seemed as if she were curled up under the blankets. No one taking a cursory glance would suspect that the real Roseanna had flown from her cage.

"Ready now?" he asked.

"Yes," Roseanna answered.

Count Czarski swung himself outside and onto the ladder.

"Give me the lantern," he ordered.

Roseanna handed it to him.

"Don't forget to shut the window behind you," he exhorted before he started down with the lantern between his teeth.

"I won't," Roseanna promised.

She followed him, closing the window sash as carefully as she could.

"I hope it doesn't open!" she prayed fervently.

Mrs. Poulet knocked lightly on the door of the billiard room.

"Roseanna!" she called softly. "Are you awake?"

Silence.

"It sounds as though she is asleep," Mr. Sandford commented.

"Yes," Evelina agreed.

"I don't want to wake her," Mrs. Poulet remarked.

"Of course not," Mr. Sandford stated.

"Shall we go, then?" Evelina inquired.

Mrs. Poulet pursed her lips undecidedly.

"If we stay, we might make a noise and disturb her," Evelina pointed out.

Mrs. Poulet frowned. "I'll try again," she said.

"Very wise," Mr. Sandford murmured.

"Roseanna!" Mrs. Poulet repeated. "Are you awake?"

Once more silence greeted her.

"She must be asleep," Evelina said.

"Not necessarily," Mr. Sandford returned. "She could be sulking."

"Not Roseanna," Evelina defended. "If she doesn't answer, she is asleep."

"I shall unlock the door and have a look anyway," Mrs. Poulet concluded.

She hunted for the correct key on her key ring and, having located it, fitted it into the lock.

15

The curtains of the billiard-room windows had not been drawn. By the light of the moon and of the candles they had with them, Mr. Sandford, Mrs. Poulet, and Evelina were able to discern a form in the bed which they took to be Roseanna.

Mrs. Poulet smiled. "You were right, Evelina," she remarked softly, "Roseanna did go to bed early."

"So it would appear," Mr. Sandford commented.

"Yes," Evelina murmured.

"Shall we go now?" Mr. Sandford inquired of Mrs. Poulet.

"Yes, I think so," Mrs. Poulet answered.

She started to leave, but then she felt a tiny breeze.

"Oh, dear!" she exclaimed. "Someone has left one of the windows open. Just a minute. I shall go and shut it."

As Roseanna began to descend the ladder, she wondered what would happen when everyone discovered that she had gone.

"Mama will be upset," she reflected. "And Mr. Sandford will probably be very angry."

But what about her brothers and Evelina?

"I wish I had been able to leave them a note," she thought.

Unfortunately, however, there had been nothing in the billiard room with which to write. And even if there had been, what could she have said? That she was eloping with the man she loved? Would they understand that?

Roseanna continued to take cautious, dainty steps down the ladder. She was nearly halfway to the ground when a sudden awful notion occurred to her.

"Marek hasn't proposed to me yet!" she realized with horror.

He had asked her to accompany him to America. He had asked Mrs. Poulet for her hand in marriage. He had asked her to go away with him then and there. But he had not actually asked her to be his wife.

"Suppose he didn't intend to wed her? Suppose he felt they ought to live together?

Roseanna stopped dead in her tracks.

Below her, Count Czarski was aware that she had halted. He paused and removed the lantern from between his teeth.

"What's the matter?" he questioned.

Roseanna turned her head so that she could see his face. By the light of the lantern she discerned two anxious eyes looking up at her.

"You haven't asked me to marry you yet!" she declared.

"I—" Count Czarski began.

"I am not going one step further unless you ask me in the proper manner!" Roseanna insisted.

Beneath her, Roseanna was able to perceive his expression. It was quizzical, amused, and exasperated all at once.

"I wish you had waited to remember that until we were on terra firma!" Count Czarski muttered.

Roseanna snorted. "Well, I didn't!" she exclaimed.

"Obviously not."

"Come on!" she demanded.

As she spoke, she observed his lips twitch.

"Miss Poulet," he inquired formally, "will you marry me?"

"Yes, Lord Czarski," she returned. "I consent to be your wife."

"Miss Poulet, you have made me the happiest man alive," he concluded in the same stilted tones. "Now can we go on, please, Roseanna?"

"We can," Roseanna allowed.

The ladder vibrated as Count Czarski shook with silent laughter during the rest of their descent. Roseanna herself was having difficulty in controlling a fit of the giggles as she proceeded downward. She had to remind herself to keep quiet, because they had not reached safety.

As Roseanna's foot touched the ground, Count Czarski flung his cloak over her shoulders. She uttered a contented little murmur as she snuggled into its warmth, grateful for the woolen folds that kept out the chilly night air.

She watched impatiently as Count Czarski took the ladder they had used and placed it flat on the grass. Her feeling of weariness, the lassitude which had paralyzed her earlier, had completely gone. She was excited. She wanted to sing and dance. She had never been so aware of being alive before, and she could hardly wait for the next part of their journey to begin.

"How clever of Marek to use the rear window," she thought.

There had been a slight danger of them being seen by her mother. However, Count Czarski had calculated correctly that since it was a dark and cold night, with rain threatening, Mrs. Poulet would have the dining room curtains drawn.

It was fortunate. If it had been summer, they would not have been so lucky. Count Czarski would have had to place his ladder toward the front of the house, where it would have been visible to the neighbors in North Row.

If a passerby had spotted what was going on, word would have spread like wildfire throughout the neighborhood. The gossips would be bound to have come by to inquire of Mrs. Poulet if they had noticed anything amiss, and if that had happened, Roseanna would have had no chance of escape.

Count Czarski blew out the candle in the lantern and set it on the grass beside the ladder.

"There is enough light from the street for us to see by," he explained.

"Yes," Roseanna stated, "but shouldn't someone take these things away before ... before morning?"

"No," Count Czarski responded. "We shall leave them lying where they are."

"But ..." Roseanna started anxiously.

What if one of the servants, checking to see that the windows were secured, discovered it? Suppose they raised the alarm? Suppose someone was sent after them to bring Roseanna back? What if they succeeded?

"It's all right," Count Czarski reassured her. "We'll make it."

Roseanna slipped her hand in his and walked with him toward the garden gate.

"Are you ... certain?" she queried hesitantly.

"Absolutely," he replied confidently. "I have planned this very carefully. You'll see."

Roseanna did not question him further. He sounded so positive!

"I hope he is correct," she reflected. "I can stand anything except being caught before we are married."

The idea of being recaptured, of being torn from his arms and brought to the prisonlike billiard room again, made her shudder. Her misery while she had been confined there had been so intense.

"I could not face that a second time!" she told herself.

Mrs. Poulet walked across the billiard room, found the window that was not completely closed, and shut it.

"Ready to come down now?" Mr. Sandford wanted to know.

"Yes," Mrs. Poulet answered.

She took a step toward the door and then changed her mind.

"I think I shall just go over and have a closer look," she decided.

"Don't wake her up," Evelina exhorted.

"I won't," Mrs. Poulet promised her.

She tiptoed over to the bed and put her candle on the bedside table. Gently, lovingly, she lifted the blanket off of what she thought was Roseanna's face so that her daughter could breathe. Then she gasped in horror: There was no face! No Roseanna!

Mr. Sandford frowned as he saw Mrs. Poulet go rigid and stare at the form in the bed in shocked silence.

"What is it?" he queried.

Mrs. Poulet was too stunned to respond.

In a trice, Mr. Sandford bounded to her side.

"What is it?" he repeated.

Mrs. Poulet found her voice.

"It is not Roseanna!" she screamed.

"Good Lord!" Mr. Sandford cried as he pulled the bedclothes back. "It ... it's a trick!"

Evelina came to the bed to see. There was Roseanna's nightdress, painstakingly arranged in her favorite sleeping position. But Roseanna herself was nowhere to be seen.

"She's gone!" Mrs. Poulet wailed. "She's gone! She's gone!"

Mr. Sandford swore an oath. Evelina gazed in awe.

"How could she have got out of here?" Mr. Sandford demanded.

Instead of answering him, Mrs. Poulet sank onto the bed, sobbing hysterically.

Evelina offered her aunt her smelling salts, but Mrs. Poulet refused them.

"This is Lord Czarski's doing!" Mr. Sandford declared. "He must have come here with a ladder and taken her out through the window."

"She'll fall and hurt herself!" Mrs. Poulet shrieked.

"Don't worry!" Mr. Sandford returned. "Roseanna

will not be hurt! Come! Let us go downstairs. We'll soon find her! Never fear. And when we do, Lord Czarski will regret his dastardly actions! That I swear!"

Hurriedly, the three of them made their way through the house and out into the garden, where Mr. Sandford quickly discovered the ladder and the lantern.

"They can't have had much of a head start!" he exclaimed. "This is still warm!"

Evelina touched the glass. "He's right," she murmured, grimacing.

"Don't fret, my dear!" Mr. Sandford exhorted. "I shall bring your daughter back to you ... unwed!"

"Is it possible?" Mrs. Poulet questioned. "Can you catch them?"

"Of course!" Mr. Sandford replied with conviction. "There is plenty of time to stop them before they reach Gretna Green! And when I lay my hands on him, Lord Czarski will rue this night's work. Mark my words!"

Mr. Sandford's lightest, fastest two-horse gig was sent for, and Mr. Sandford had himself driven along North Row at a rare pace.

"Take the road for Gretna Green!" Mr. Sandford ordered as his coachman reached the junction of North Row and Park Lane. "Hurry!"

They traveled along the Edgeware Road in a northwesterly direction. Only a couple of minutes had elapsed when Mr. Sandford spotted a cumbersome hackney carriage, of the sort anyone might hire, ahead of him. As his gig drew closer, a man and a woman poked their heads inquiringly out of the windows. No sooner did they catch sight of Mr. Sandford than they had their own horses speed up.

"After them!" Mr. Sandford roared. "After them! Don't let them get away!"

His coachman obeyed instantly. Faster and faster the horses went. With every foot of ground they covered, they gained on the fugitives.

"Any second now we'll have them!" Mr. Sandford thought.

Then, suddenly, the conveyance he was pursuing rounded the corner and, without warning, an identical one appeared alongside it, in front of him.

Mr. Sandford was nonplussed. Both vehicles were driving at great speed northwards, churning up clouds of dust behind them and obscuring his view. In order to block him further, they frequently went from one side of the road to the other, so that he became confused as to which was the original.

It did not help matters that the hackney carriages were so similar. In addition, the moon was now hidden by clouds and it was drizzling.

"Botheration!" Mr. Sandford exclaimed.

They had just passed the outskirts of London. From here on, there would be no street lamps to light the way. That meant this part of the road was pitch-dark.

"I must make a move," Mr. Sandford decided.

"The one on the left!" he told his coachman. "Corner the one on the left!"

As they came to within sight of the first inn beyond the metropolis, Mr. Sandford's gig swooped on the conveyance, which slowed to a standstill.

With a mighty bound. Mr. Sandford leaped down and opened the door. No Count Czarski. No Roseanna. No one at all, in fact. The hackney carriage was empty.

"Damn and blast it!" Mr. Sandford swore fiercely.

They had been in pursuit of the wrong vehicle!

"The other one!" Mr. Sandford commanded. "Quick! We must catch it!"

"Sir, the horses!" his coachman protested. "They are worn out!"

Mr. Sandford had only to glance at the poor beasts to see that his servant was correct. They were foaming at the mouth and steam was rising from their flanks. They could not possibly continue the race.

"Get fresh ones!" Mr. Sandford ordered.

"Sir?" the coachman asked blankly.

In the middle of the night?

"Rouse the ostlers! Have them harness a post chaise!" Mr. Sandford cried impatiently. "No! Better still, get me a horse for myself. Hire a horse for me, dammit, man! Hurry up! Look lively! Don't stand there dithering!"

In less than five minutes, a horse was procured and

148

saddled. And Mr. Sandford, who was no mean rider, was on his way once more.

Although he had lost time, he soon made it up, and within minutes he had his quarry in sight again.

Mr. Sandford did not consider it strange that the hackney carriage he was chasing had turned round and was heading back to London. It did not strike him as odd that the horses pulling it had not tired as quickly as his own. He continued to bear down on the runaways with unyielding determination. Faster and faster he went, urging his mount to gallop like the wind, in his eagerness to capture the luckless pair.

"We are coming to North Row!" Mr. Sandford realized.

He gave a whoop of triumph. He may have erred in choosing which vehicle to apprehend, but his presence had succeeded in its object.

"Lord Czarski has got cold feet," he told himself. "He is going to take Roseanna home!"

Mr. Sandford smiled. He knew what had unnerved the Pole. Count Czarski was frightened of being charged with kidnapping an heiress, and he was about to give her up. Of course, it was only to be expected. These foreigners! Spineless, the lot of them!

Then, as Mr. Sandford prepared to close in on the fugitives, another hackney carriage appeared out of the blue and, as before, his path was blocked.

"Aha! I know what they are doing!" Mr. Sandford informed his horse. "Transferring from one carriage to the other when the two are near enough together! That's why the horses are fresh!"

He could see it being done. A man and a woman, obviously Roseanna and Count Czarski, stepped from the first conveyance to the second as they hurtled along, side by side.

Mr. Sandford winced as he watched what was happening:

"That is dangerous!" he muttered. "How can he permit her to do it?"

He urged his horse on in pursuit.

"I suppose they hoped they could elude me this way," he reflected.

However, distracting though it had been, Mr. Sandford was onto their little game now, and he resolved not to allow them to escape. He would catch them. Never fear!

"The swine!" Mr. Sandford added, referring to Count Czarski, as he followed the equipage from Grosvenor Square, where the switch had taken place, along Brook Street. "I had no idea he could be so inconsiderate, so careless of Roseanna's safety!"

The vehicle bearing the fleeing couple clattered through Hanover Square into Swallow Street. From there it entered Carnaby Market and drove from Bread Street into Soho Square, stopping finally when it reached High Holborn.

Mr. Sandford, who had been frustrated in his attempts to overtake the miscreants by the width of their coach and the narrowness of the lanes, frowned.

He had understood the purpose behind the multiplicity of hired conveyances. The fugitives had intended to shake him off. If they had had more time, it would have worked. But they had been unfortunate, and they had failed to do so.

Keeping to the back streets had certain advantages as well. Mr. Sandford was skillfully detained behind the cumbersome hackney carriage. If the changeover had succeeded, he would have been pinned down while Roseanna and Count Czarski made their getaway in the newly arrived vehicle with the fresh horses.

Thus far, their plan was comprehensible to Mr. Sandford. They relied on creating confusion in order to give any pursuers the slip.

But now they were proceeding along the grand thoroughfare of High Holborn. That broke the pattern, and Mr. Sandford could not see the point.

"What are they playing at?" he asked himself.

Abruptly, he saw it: A fourth carriage emerged from Furnival's Inn.

Mr. Sandford swore unrestrainedly. He had never used so much bad language in his entire life. He had barely enough time to procure a fresh horse from the startled ostlers and to set off after the couple once more.

"This is it!" he thought.

They were no longer in a hackney carriage but in a swift post chaise. No more games—this was the real thing.

"It's now or never!" Mr. Sandford reflected. "If I lose them..."

He dug his spur into his mount's flank. Ahead of him, he could just see the post chaise tearing along High Holborn, and into Oxford Street.

"The tollgate might slow them down," Mr. Sandford told himself.

The post chaise was being driven due west. That meant that it would soon come to the turnpike on the site of the Tyburn gallows.

Yes! They were making for it!

Mr. Sandford's smile was grim. This was his last chance to catch them, and he urged his horse to go faster still

The guardian of the tollgate was sound asleep in his bed. The occupants of the post chaise had to rouse him and persuade him to accept his due as well as to unfasten the barrier for them.

Suddenly Mr. Sandford drew up beside them. He bared his teeth and laughed malevolently. There was not another vehicle in sight!

"I have you now!" he declared with malicious glee. "You shall not escape me this time!"

16

Count Czarski took Roseanna to where he had a carriage waiting. It was only a short walk away from the front gate, hidden from view of the house by the hedge that marked the boundary of their next-door neighbor's property.

He helped her to ascend and joined her inside. Then he lit the lantern that hung on a hook from the ceiling of the interior and signaled to the coachman to drive off.

Roseanna blinked as her surroundings were illuminated. She had never been in so luxurious a vehicle. White satin lining. Thick velvet curtains to shelter the occupants from the vulgar gaze of the hoi polloi. Brocade ceiling.

"What a magnificent carriage!" she exclaimed.

"I'm glad you like it," Count Czarski answered.

"It's beautiful. Was it very expensive?"

"I don't know."

"You don't know!"

"No. It isn't mine, you see. I borrowed it."

"Borrowed it?" Roseanna echoed.

"Yes."

Roseanna eyed him apprehensively, wondering if the word might not be a euphemism for something else.

Count Czarski smiled. "It's all right, I didn't steal it," he assured her. "My grandmother lent it to me."

"Ah!" Roseanna breathed.

Count Czarski pulled a wicker basket out from under the seat.

"Here," he said, handing the hamper to her. "Now you can have supper."

Roseanna, who was famished, was delighted, and she ate ravenously.

Count Czarski watched her indulgently.

"You look like someone who has been starved for a week," he remarked.

"I feel it!" Roseanna cried.

"Was that room so terrible for you, then?"

"Yes!"

As she said the word, his arm went around her.

"It was horrible," she elaborated. "I've never hated any place so much. I..."

He put his finger on her lips, silencing her.

"Forget it," he ordered. "It is past. You will never have to go back there again."

Roseanna curled up in his arms. She was completely comfortable and at ease. Only one thing was troubling her.

"How did you know where I was?" she queried. "How did you find out what had happened?"

He drew her still closer and kissed her neck, making her spine tingle.

"I guessed that we might be in for something of the sort," he stated. "When I went to ask your mother for your hand in marriage this afternoon, I had a feeling she would refuse."

"Then why did you do it?"

"I had to try."

"Oh."

"Anyway," he continued, "I surmised that she would

153

probably say no and that you and she would fall out over her obduracy."

"Hmmmmm," Roseanna murmured. "Was that why you didn't stop to talk to me?"

Count Czarski frowned. "I didn't see you when I visited," he responded. "Where were you?"

"I was coming down the stairs with Evelina," Roseanna told him. "I called out to you, but you left the house so fast..."

"Oh. I'm sorry. I would have taken you with me then and there if I had realized. But perhaps it is better this way."

"Perhaps," Roseanna conceded.

It was very pleasant traveling like this. She knew exactly how cats must feel, lying in their baskets before a nice warm fire. Deliciously cozy!

"But how did you learn where I was?" she wondered after a while.

"I have your dear cousin Evelina to thank for that," he informed her.

"Really?"

"Yes, really."

Roseanna half sat up and turned round to look at him.

"What do you mean, Marek?" she inquired.

By way of a reply, Count Czarski reached into his breast pocket and handed Roseanna an envelope with a letter inside.

"I don't know when she wrote this or how she hoped to convey it to me," he said as Roseanna began to peruse it. "My servant Tomasz brought it to me early this evening. He told me that he had met Evelina quite by chance in Bond Street and that she had pushed it into his hand, giving him to understand that it was for me."

"I thought he didn't speak English."

"He doesn't. Fortunately, though he could not fathom what Evelina was saying, she happened to mention my name, and he deduced that she wanted him to take the letter to me. He also gathered from her tone that it was urgent, so he came hurrying to the Albany with it immediately."

"That was lucky!"

154

"Yes, wasn't it," Count Czarski agreed.

Roseanna glanced down at the note:

Dear Marek [Evelina had written]

Aunt has locked Roseanna in the billiard room—that funny tower on the side of our house—without food. I've never seen her (Aunt, that is) in such a temper. I'm afraid Roseanna will either have to face starvation or promise never to set eyes on you again. I can't help her, as Aunt won't listen to reason and Mr. Sandford backs her up in everything. Do something!

Yours, Evelina Poulet.

P.S. Burn this.

"But you have not burnt it!" Roseanna protested.

"No. Not yet. But I will," Count Czarski promised. "I wanted you to see it first."

"Oh."

Roseanna folded it up and returned it to him. For five minutes or so neither of them spoke, and then he asked:

"Do you want any more to eat?"

"No, thank you," Roseanna answered.

"Are you sure you have had enough?"

"Yes, thank you. I have had plenty."

"In that case, I think we should both try to get some sleep," he stated. "We have a long journey ahead of us."

"Yes. Very well," Roseanna concurred.

Count Czarski ordered the coach to stop and handed the wicker basket to his servant Tomasz, who was, as Roseanna saw to her surprise, their coachman for that night.

A few seconds was all it needed to transform the two seats into a bed. By placing the cushions from the back in the center where one normally put one's legs, and by lifting up a flap at one end, revealing a cubbyhole where one could put one's feet, one was provided with sufficient room to stretch out and lie down.

Roseanna gave a cry of delight at the ingenuity of construction, as the count lifted her up onto the makeshift bed and covered the two of them with a luxuriant fur cloak.

"It is marvelous!" she declared.

"Isn't it?" he agreed.

"Whose idea was it?"

"My grandmother's. She hates traveling by carriage. The only way she will consent to do it is to lie flat. I don't know whether she gets any sleep on her journeys or not, but she insists that every carriage she owns be designed like this, so that she can rest if she wishes to."

"How clever of her!" Roseanna cried.

Count Czarski smiled.

Roseanna lay down. There were no pillows, and when she put her head back she found it resting on his arm.

"Sleep well," he whispered.

"You too," she returned.

Mr. Sandford strode over to the post chaise at the turnpike and exultantly threw open the door. Then, to his dismay, he discovered that the man and woman inside the vehicle he had been following were not the count and Roseanna, but complete strangers. Even worse, they had been deliberately leading him astray.

In questioning the decoys, Mr. Sandford learned that they had been hired by Count Czarski for the express purpose of keeping him—that is, Mr. Sandford—running around in circles for as long as possible. They had been paid a fairly substantial sum to deceive him into pursuing them north, then east, and finally west.

Mr. Sandford's hatred of Count Czarski increased. He had never approved of the man, and now the wretch had made him look like an idiot. It was insupportable!

Furthermore, he discovered that the couple, who were professional circus tumblers, had been promised a bonus—which, alas, they had now lost—if they could keep him chasing them from midnight until dawn.

Mr. Sandford's wounded pride was a little assuaged on hearing that he had caught up with the acrobats after a shorter time than Count Czarski had bargained on. However, he was very angry and not a bit sympathetic toward the entertainers.

Mr. Sandford acknowledged that he had been outmaneuvred by Count Czarski, and he did not relish the prospect of having to admit it on his arrival in North Row. But, he reasoned, at least Roseanna had not been subjected to this hazardous ride! That was a small consolation!

Mr. Sandford dismissed the decoys with the contumeley he felt they deserved for their part in Count Czarski's deception and made his way back to North Row.

"How am I going to tell Mrs. Poulet?" he wondered. "How is she going to take it?"

It was after midnight by now, but neither Mrs. Poulet nor Evelina had been able to sleep, and they met Mr. Sandford as he came through the front door.

"Did you ... ?" Mrs. Poulet began hopefully. And then, seeing Mr. Sandford was alone, she added, "Oh. No. You didn't get her."

"No," Mr. Sandford replied, hanging his head. "I'm sorry. But Lord Czarski is—er—more—er—devious than I originally anticipated. I had no idea that he could be so cunning or so sly!"

"What do you mean?" Evelina inquired, puzzled.

"He had carriages ready to lead me on a wild-goose chase," Mr. Sandford explained. "I pursued a couple I thought were Roseanna and Lord Czarski north toward Gretna Green, then east and then west. When I caught up with them at the turnpike I discovered they were hired acrobats!"

"No!" Evelina exclaimed.

"Incredible, isn't it?" Mr. Sandford demanded rhetorically. "I cannot convey to you what a fool I was made to look!"

"Poor Mr. Sandford!" Evelina cried. "What a thing to happen!"

Mrs. Poulet dabbed her eyes, which were red from weeping.

"Have you no idea where Roseanna is?" she asked tragically.

"None whatsoever," Mr. Sandford answered. "At

first I believed they would make for Gretna Green. But now I am not sure."

"I don't suppose . . ." Evelina started.

"Yes?" Mrs. Poulet prompted as her niece hesitated.

". . . Is it possible that Denis might know?" Evelina completed.

"That is an excellent suggestion, young lady!" Mr. Sandford declared, brightening. "I shall go straight to the Albany and see if he can be of assistance!"

Evelina bit her lip. "Oh, I hope Marek hasn't told Denis his plans!" she reflected worriedly. "Why couldn't I keep my big mouth shut?"

On the other hand, she comforted herself, Count Czarski did have a two-hour or more head start.

"And besides," she reckoned, "if I hadn't mentioned Denis, one of the others would have done so sooner or later."

It was better that she had spoken when she did. If she had not done so, her part in the elopement might have been exposed.

". . . and that must never happen!"

Mr. Sandford's coachman had returned to North Row with the gig, drawn by fresh horses, and was thus able to drive his master directly to Denis Martin's flat.

Since it was by then the early hours of the morning, there were few carriages in the streets and nothing impeded Mr. Sandford's progress. He had to wake the startled porter at the Albany, to whom he announced that it was a matter of life and death, but he was soon admitted to the private apartments.

Within seconds, he was up the stairs and banging on the door.

Denis Martin heard the noise. He had been in a deep sleep, dreaming pleasantly, when Mr. Sandford arrived. He roused himself with difficulty and stumbled into the hallway, muttering about the lack of consideration of some people.

"Who on earth can be making such a commotion in the middle of the night?" he wondered.

As he opened the door, bleary-eyed and not fully awake, he caught sight of Mr. Sandford.

"Good Lord!" he exclaimed. "What are you doing here?"

Mr. Sandford pushed Denis unceremoniously into the sitting room and closed the door with a snap behind him.

"What am *I* doing here?" he countered agitatedly. "How can you ask such a question? What are *you* doing here?"

Denis Martin lowered himself into a chair.

"What?" he responded, bewildered. "But I *live* here!"

"Then you must be aware of what has happened!" Mr. Sandford declared in outraged tones. "And—"

"Pardon?" Denis interposed.

Mr. Sandford ignored the interruption.

"—and you jolly well ought to be out doing something about it!" he concluded.

Denis Martin blinked at his visitor in astonishment.

"Are you, by any chance...intoxicated?" he inquired.

"Certainly not!" Mr. Sandford barked crossly.

"Pity," Denis replied forlornly.

"Really, sir!"

"Yes it is. You see, if you had been drunk, I should have understood and offered you a nice hot cup of strong black coffee. Works wonders, you know. But as it is, I haven't a clue as to what is going on."

"You haven't?"

"Not the slightest."

"Are you sure?"

"Positive. Unless..."

"Yes?"

"*I* haven't been drinking, have I?"

Mr. Sandford sniffed his host's breath.

"No," he adjudicated decisively.

"Oh. Shame."

"Why?"

"If I were, I would be able to fathom my inability to comprehend."

"Are you serious?"

"Perfectly."

"You really have no idea what's the matter?"

"None."

"Then it will come as something of a shock to you, I fear," Mr. Sandford told him solemnly.

"Oh?" Denis Martin questioned uneasily. "What is it?"

"Your dear friend Lord Czarski has eloped with your cousin Roseanna."

"I . . . I . . . I don't believe it!" Denis Martin gasped.

"It is true," Mr. Sandford reiterated. "They have run off together."

Denis Martin's face drained of color. It was one thing to ask your aunt to consider the request of a certain nobleman for her daughter's hand in marriage. It was quite another, where permission to wed had been refused, to countenance two people absconding in that fashion.

Denis was now wide awake. He leaped to his feet and charged into Count Czarski's bedroom. There, propped up on the pillows, he found a note. It said simply:

I have gone to examine the ship I am having built at Portsmouth to sail for America. Back in four or five weeks. Look after yourself. Marek.

It was enough to confirm Mr. Sandford's allegations. Denis leaned on the doorpost.

"Oh, no!" he groaned. "How could he!"

"You see!" Mr. Sandford exclaimed, feeling vindicated at last. "I was right! The man's a blackguard!"

Denis could not disagree with him. According to the attitudes of the day, eloping constituted a serious crime—treason against parental authority. No gentleman would contemplate such a thing. Denis himself shuddered at the very notion. If this escapade failed, there was disgrace and humiliation in store for the young lady concerned. If it succeeded, her parents could well charge the man with kidnapping an heiress. The danger! The ignominy! The scandal!

"Have you considered pursuing them?" Denis asked in a choked voice.

"Yes, I have," Mr. Sandford answered, "but apparently your dear friend had anticipated my action, and sent me on a wild-goose chase."

"Oh."

"You didn't suspect what he was up to?"

Denis shook his head in negation.

"I was out for most of the day and most of the evening as well," he explained. "I came in at six and Marek told me he was going to retire early."

"Hah!"

"I saw no reason to disbelieve him," Denis defended. "I had no notion he was planning to run off with Roseanna. And when I returned from the Ravenshaws', I assumed he was asleep. It was nearly midnight then, you know!"

"I see. So you saw him last at six in the evening."

"No," Denis corrected. "At seven, when I finished changing."

"Hrmph!" Mr. Sandford snorted.

"When did you discover Roseanna was missing?"

"Shortly after ten. Mrs. Poulet was worried about her daughter and she went upstairs to check on her."

"Worried?" Denis Martin interrogated. "Why?"

Mr. Sandford reminded him how Count Czarski had come to request Roseanna's hand in marriage earlier that day but had been turned down. Following Denis Martin's own departure, Roseanna and her mother had had words.

"Mrs. Poulet felt that her daughter's attitude was particularly reprehensible," Mr. Sandford stated. "Therefore she decided to teach her a lesson."

It needed only a little probing for Denis Martin to ferret out the fact that Mrs. Poulet had shut Roseanna in the billiard room without any supper, and that it was much later in the evening when his aunt had started to show concern for her daughter and had insisted on going up to see that Roseanna was all right.

"That's when we found out about this ghastly business," Mr. Sandford said.

Denis Martin put his head in his hands.

"Oh, no!" he moaned.

Of course Count Czarski would not take no for an answer, especially not if Mrs. Poulet had been rude. And naturally Roseanna resented being treated like a prisoner.

If he, Denis, had known the whole story, he would have guessed that an elopement was imminent. Then he would have stuck to the count like glue, and been ready to prevent it—for everyone's sake.

But it was too late to stop it now. Or was it?

Denis Martin glanced at the clock to gauge how much of a head start the fugitives had had.

"Great heavens!" he cried. "It is half past two!"

Roseanna and Count Czarski had a four-and-a-half-hour lead at the very least.

"Yes," Mr. Sandford agreed, following his train of thought. "Time is running out! Unless we catch them, I fear that Lord Czarski may persuade Roseanna to go through some kind of sham ceremony, thus making her believe that they are legally married."

Denis Martin was shocked. "I don't think Marek would do that," he replied. "It is not his style."

"Indeed? Not even if he wanted revenge on her family and her friends?"

Denis Martin frowned. "Why should he desire that?" he questioned.

"Because we exposed him."

"Are you referring to your discovery that you were mistaken about his nationality? That instead of being Russian, he was Polish?"

"Exactly."

Denis sighed. "Marek isn't the type to wreak vengeance for something like that," he insisted, "particularly not on the weak or the helpless."

"Hrmph! Well, perhaps not," Mr. Sandford conceded, "but in that case, have you any idea where he might take her to marry her legally?"

"No. None. Don't you know where they have gone?"

"I haven't the faintest notion. At first I believed they would make for Gretna Green, but ..."

"Most unlikely," Denis interrupted. "Marek is a

Pole, remember. He doesn't know much about England—or Scotland either, come to that."

"So I discovered," Mr. Sandford continued acidly. "He had a number of hackney carriages ready to lead me on a wild-goose chase. I went after them, like an idiot, north along the Edgeware Road, east to High Holborn, and west to Tyburn before I discovered the deception."

"Oh, dear," Denis murmured.

"Well might you say 'Oh, dear'!" Mr. Sandford hissed. "Do you still feel sure he intends to make her his wife?"

"Yes. Whatever Marek is up to, it does not include humiliating Roseanna with a mock wedding."

"Hmmmm. Very well. We'll say no more about that. But I sincerely hope you are correct."

"So do I," Denis Martin replied with feeling. He grimaced. "I suppose I had better get dressed and come back with you to see Aunt."

"That might help," Mr. Sandford agreed.

Denis repaired to his bedroom to attire himself. As soon as he was ready, the two men went to North Row, where Mrs. Poulet and Evelina were waiting for them.

"I can't tell you what a terrible night this has been!" Mrs. Poulet exclaimed as she ushered her nephew and Mr. Sandford into the drawing room. "I have never wept so copiously in my life! I declare, I have no more tears left to shed!"

"I am sorry, Aunt," Denis apologized. "I had no inkling that anything like this would happen."

"Nor had I," Evelina added. "I don't imagine any of us guessed."

"You are correct there," Mr. Sandford seconded. "Who would have credited that the poor innocent child could have been so dominated by Lord Czarski that she would run away from her loving family?"

"Oh, don't!" Mrs. Poulet wailed. "You'll break my heart if you go on like that!"

"We must get them back!" Mr. Sandford insisted.

"But how?" Evelina wondered. "Do *you* know where they have gone?"

Denis Martin, to whom her question had been addressed, shook his head in negation.

At this Mrs. Poulet gave a despairing cry and sank down onto the sofa, where Mr. Sandford joined her. Denis lowered himself into an armchair, while Evelina draped herself becomingly across another one.

For several seconds, silence reigned.

"I have been thinking," Denis Martin remarked eventually. "I believe I have discovered where Marek has taken Roseanna."

17

Roseanna heard a voice calling her gently out of her slumber. She opened her eyes and found herself gazing up at the count.

"It is morning," he told her. "We shall stop for breakfast soon."

Roseanna frowned, puzzled. "Morning?" she asked. "Where am I?"

And what, pray, was *he* doing there?

"In my grandmother's carriage," Count Czarski reminded her, "eloping with me."

At once her memory returned.

"Oh, yes," she responded. "I couldn't think where I was for a moment. Yes, let's stop for breakfast."

"I shall tell Tomasz, then," Count Czarski replied, and he gave his servant orders to halt at the next inn.

"Did you sleep well?" Count Czarski inquired later.

"Mmmm, yes," Roseanna murmured. "I was having such a lovely dream when you woke me."

"There will be more of them," Count Czarski promised her as he leaned over and kissed her.

"Did *you* sleep well?"

"Yes," he answered softly.

Presently their carriage drew in at a hostelry in a small but prosperous-looking town. Count Czarski climbed out first and helped Roseanna to descend.

"What's the matter?" he questioned as she grimaced.

"I'm still wearing the dress I had on yesterday," she stated. "I wish I could change."

"That is easily arranged."

"Is it?"

"Of course. You can put something else on whenever you want. I'll hire a room for you."

"I can? But how, Marek?" she queried. "I have only got this!"

She had come with him literally in the clothes she stood up in. She had taken nothing. How could she possibly array herself in fresh attire?

Count Czarski smiled curiously at her.

"Before we embarked on this journey," he explained, "I bought you a couple of gowns. Of course, I don't know whether or not they will fit, but you can try them on if you like."

"Oh," Roseanna said. "Thank you. You seem to have thought of everything."

"I try to," he returned, raising her hand to his lips.

He booked two rooms at the inn, so that they could both change before they dined.

With the assistance of the maid at the inn, Roseanna dressed in one of the dresses he had purchased for her. It proved to be an excellent fit.

"How did he manage to guess my size so accurately?" she wondered.

And where had he found a garment that was ready made?

Roseanna came out of her room to discover Count Czarski waiting for her on the landing. Instead of a formal city suit, he wore a more casual outfit in the fashionable "parsley mixture" color, in which he contrived to appear every inch a gentleman.

"How did you know my size?" Roseanna asked when they were seated at breakfast.

Count Czarski smiled. "I have always been able to guess a woman's measurements," he replied. "My father was the same. He could assess precisely what would fit my mother and what wouldn't."

"Oh," Roseanna commented. "But where did you buy it? I mean ... it is completely finished. How ...?"

"That was a piece of luck."

"What do you mean?"

"Yesterday, when I was making the arrangements for us to get away safely, I noticed a girl serving in a shop who looked the same build as you," he explained, "and I asked her if I could buy a dress of hers for you."

"And ... and she agreed?" Roseanna gasped.

After all, it was hardly the sort of request that gentlemen customarily made to shopgirls!

"Yes," Count Czarski said. "Well ... when I told her why I wanted it, she consented to let me have those two."

Roseanna's eyebrows rose. "What did you tell her, Marek?" she demanded primly.

Count Czarski looked guilty. "I am afraid I invented a story for her," he confessed.

"What was it?"

"That my poor wife had lost every stitch of clothing she possessed in a fire that very afternoon and—"

Roseanna started to laugh. "Oh you are terrible, Marek!" she declared.

"Don't complain. You have your dresses, at any rate," he pointed out.

"Yes," Roseanna concurred. "I am glad about that."

When breakfast was over, they continued on their journey in a hired post chaise. The carriage, with its impromptu bed, came behind them with a coachman driving and Tomasz resting inside, for, as Marek said, he needed sleep too; he could not be expected, old as he was, to work for so long without pause.

As they traversed the bumpy roads, it occurred to Roseanna to wonder whether or not they were being pursued.

"Do you think we will be followed, Marek?" she questioned.

"Without doubt," he replied. "That is why we have to go on traveling throughout the night tonight as well as all day. I hope you don't mind."

"No. I don't mind. Who will come after us?"

Count Czarski shrugged noncommittally.

"Who knows?" he countered. "The army? The navy? The Bow Street Runners, perhaps?"

"Marek!" Roseanna cried alarmed. "You are not serious!"

"No. No. I am not serious."

"Well, who do you really believe will chase us?"

"Mr. Sandford probably, and maybe Denis as well."

"Oh." There was a long pause and then Roseanna queried: "What do you suppose they are doing now?"

"Trying to digest their breakfasts, no doubt."

"Oh, don't be such a tease!"

"It is you who are the tease," Count Czarski contradicted.

"I?" Roseanna asked blankly. "What do you mean?"

Count Czarski smiled in that curious way that Roseanna did not understand and kissed her lightly.

"Sometimes you are so innocent that it is unbelievable!" he murmured.

Roseanna's brows furrowed and she stared at him in bewilderment. She had not a clue as to what he was talking about. It never crossed her mind that he was referring to the fact that she had lain in his arms the entire night and yet he had not taken her.

"The meals they give us here are much too large," Roseanna said when they stopped for lunch. "I can't eat any more."

"You are not compelled to," Count Czarski returned. "I shall not force you . . . to do anything."

Once again, Roseanna failed to see that there was another meaning hidden in his words.

"You know," Count Czarski mused when they reentered the post chaise, "I've been thinking. . . ."

"Yes?" Roseanna prompted.

"It might be nice, to pass the time, if I taught you Polish."

Roseanna looked stricken.

"What's the matter?"

"Er...well...nothing...only I've never been any good at languages," she admitted.

"No? You speak French, so Denis tells me. And fairly fluently at that."

"Um...yes...but...I always hated my French lessons, and—"

Count Czarski silenced her objections with a kiss.

"This won't be like learning French in school, believe me," he told her.

"You promise?"

"I promise."

"And if I find it is too difficult, we can stop?"

"Of course."

Roseanna's relief was plainly evident.

"Oh, good!" she exclaimed. "Because my French lessons were so interminably long and I could not abide those boring French verb drills."

"I won't give you anything like that."

"Fine. But Marek?"

"Yes?"

"Why...why do you want me to study Polish? After all, you said you could never return—"

She stopped speaking abruptly. For a moment she had seen a shaft of intense pain flash through his eyes. Even such a brief glimpse of him suffering tore her apart inside.

"Why didn't I keep that to myself?" she demanded silently.

"No. I can't ever go back...home," Count Czarski responded softly. "But I have been considering what it will be like in America. According to my sister and my brothers, there are many Polish people there. Few of them were able to learn English before they arrived, and those who know my family come to them to ask them for help."

"What sort of help?"

"They wish to have things translated for them."

169

Roseanna frowned. "I...I don't understand," she stated.

"As a nobleman, I was brought up to accept that I had certain obligations to fulfill," Count Czarski explained. "I was bound to protect my people in wartime, for instance. In exchange for carrying out these duties, we, members of the aristocracy like myself, received certain privileges."

"I don't follow."

"Patience."

"Sorry."

"All my life I have been loyally supported by my people. You have only to observe my servant Tomasz. His devotion has gone far beyond that of a mere employee."

"Hmmmmm. Ye-es."

"Since I have been given so much, I feel I owe it to my people to repay what I can."

Roseanna's brow furrowed. She still did not see what he was driving at.

"Although, when I go to America, I shall have to give up my title," he continued, "I shall still be 'Count Czarski' for many Poles..."

Roseanna nodded in assent. He had told her that since America was a republic they would have to surrender their distinctions and revert to using simple forms of address.

"...and they will come to me automatically for assistance," Count Czarski concluded, "as they would have done in Poland."

"Yes," Roseanna murmured.

"They may have difficulty in understanding their new language," he went on. "The men may come to me with their legal problems and the women may call on you to find out the right name for the meat or the curtain material they propose to purchase."

"Yes," Roseanna agreed.

As his countess, she would be required to do her share. Even though she relinquished the honor, she would naturally have to support her husband to return whatever it was he felt was due to his people.

"But what if I can't learn Polish?" she asked. "What if it is too difficult for me?"

Count Czarski smiled and kissed her.

"I don't expect you to master it in a few hours," he assured her. "It will take a long time to become fluent. But you forget, there is our voyage to the United States. We shall have an excellent opportunity then."

"But—" Roseanna protested.

"Don't worry," he cut in. "Even if you know merely a few phrases, it will be a help."

Roseanna was thoughtful. "Yes, I suppose so," she mused.

She was not entirely happy about the idea. Her experiences with French had put her off the notion of studying another tongue.

However, Count Czarski's methods were nothing like the ones she had endured as a child. First he gave her some words to memorize, pronouncing them slowly and distinctly so that she could understand them, then showing her how to write them down, then asking her to repeat them.

Patiently, he coaxed her to say *hello, good-bye, yes, please, no,* and *thank you* in Polish. Next, he progressed to useful nouns. By the end of the day, he had even taught her one of those dreaded verbs, so that she could form simple sentences, albeit with difficulty.

Count Czarski praised Roseanna lavishly for her efforts, so that she soon overcame her fear of failing or of looking foolish and became interested in this strange new speech. She listened fascinated as unusual combinations of sounds issued from his lips.

"Tell me more," she begged him.

"No. Let's stop. You must be tired," he responded.

"I'm not. I'm not. Give me another sentence, please."

He smiled. "Very well," he agreed. "If you are certain it is not too much."

"I'm sure."

"All right then," he conceded. "Say '*Ja cię kocham.*'"

"That's difficult!" Roseanna exclaimed.

The nasal sounds seemed impossible to utter!

"I'll write it down for you," he stated.

Roseanna gazed at the phrase, frowning with intense concentration as she did so.

"Now repeat it," he instructed. *"Ja cię kocham."*

"Ja cię kocham," Roseanna echoed.

As she concluded, she glanced at him to see if she had done well or not. There was a peculiar expression on his face which she did not comprehend.

"What's the matter?" she asked.

"Nothing," Count Czarski answered.

"Didn't I pronounce it properly?"

"Oh, yes. Beautifully."

"But?" Roseanna prompted.

"But? But nothing."

"Marek, is there something wrong with that sentence?"

"No. Not a thing."

Still that odd gleam had not departed from his eyes. Roseanna tilted her head to one side.

"It is rude, isn't it Marek?" she challenged. "You have made me say some rude words!"

"Roseanna! Really!" Count Czarski was quite shocked. "How could you think such a thing?"

Roseanna pouted at him.

"It is polite, believe me," he assured her, "only . . ."

"Yes?" Roseanna questioned.

"You said it as if you did not mean it."

"What does it mean, then?"

"What does what mean, then?" Count Czarski inquired with feigned innocence.

"Ja cię kocham," she said slowly, since the words did not come easily to her.

Count Czarski's lips twitched. "It means *I love you,*" he told her.

Roseanna colored. In an instant he had his arms around her and he began to caress her. Again and again he said that he loved her, in English, in French, and in Polish, kissing her wildly, until at last she was able to respond to him in his own tongue, telling him that she loved him, with all the passion of her soul.

18

"Yes?" Mrs. Poulet asked eagerly. "Where do you think he has taken her?"

"Yes, where?" Evelina wondered.

"Tell us!" Mr. Sandford demanded.

"You remember, Mr. Sandford, you said that Marek had sent decoy carriages north along the Edgeware Road," Denis inquired, "making you believe they were going to Gretna Green?"

"I recall," Mr. Sandford replied.

"Then you followed the acrobats east towards Holborn?"

"Yes."

"And finally west to Tyburn?"

"Correct."

"But at no time did any one of the vehicles you pursued go due south."

"Exactly."

"You are sure?"

"Absolutely," Mr. Sandford answered, "unless you

count the fact that the one I encountered in the Edge-ware Road turned back to North Row before it proceeded east. But no. The circus people whom Lord Czar-ski hired confessed that they had been paid to lure me north, then east, and then as far west as possible. But not south."

"Aha!" Denis Martin exclaimed. "I thought so!"

"What is it?" Mrs. Poulet questioned excitedly.

"Don't keep us in suspense!" Evelina cried.

"I believe that they have gone south," Denis Martin informed the others with conviction.

Evelina recovered from her astonishment first.

"What makes you say that?" she wanted to know.

"Because Marek tried to lead Mr. Sandford in every direction except south," Denis returned.

"I don't understand," Mrs. Poulet complained.

"When Mr. Sandford discovered Roseanna missing, he thought Marek would take her to Gretna Green; therefore, he went north," Denis clarified. "When he caught sight of the first hackney carriage, his suspicions were confirmed and he gave chase."

"Precisely," Mr. Sandford stated.

"But, as I said earlier," Denis continued, "Marek is not English, but Polish. He knows precious little about our customs. He has probably never even heard of Gretna Green."

"Do you mean the choice of direction was fortuitous on his part?" Mr. Sandford demanded.

"Not exactly," Denis responded. "No."

"What do you mean?" Mrs. Poulet inquired.

"Evelina," Denis commanded, "give me the points of the compass. Quickly!"

"North-south-east-west," Evelina answered swiftly.

"You see!" Denis Martin concluded triumphantly. "North takes precedence in everyone's mind. That's why he knew Mr. Sandford would start there. It was logical."

"Hmmmm. Yes. I see," Mr. Sandford murmured. "In other words, he relied on my selecting that route from force of habit."

"Correct. He hoped, by having the hackney carriage double back to North Row, to prevent you from noticing the discrepancy," Denis replied. "South should have come before east."

"Yes," Mr. Sandford concurred. "I agree with you so far, but—"

"One moment," Denis ordered, "and all will become clear."

"Your pardon," Mr. Sandford said.

"Granted," Denis Martin returned magnanimously.

"Do go on, Denis!" Mrs. Poulet urged. "I am on tenterhooks!"

"Me too," Evelina added.

"Marek tricked Mr. Sandford into going along every road except the one he had actually chosen," Denis explained. "So, far from marrying Roseanna in Britain, Marek intends to take her to the Continent. At this very moment he is probably on his way to Dover!"

A stunned silence followed. None of the others had considered the possibility that Count Czarski might have taken Roseanna to Europe. They had grown so accustomed to the fact of there being a war on, and thus travel abroad being sufficiently restricted as to be out of the question for ordinary people like themselves, that it had not occurred to them.

But the war was over. Only a day or two ago King Louis XVIII had gone back to France, after an exile of nearly a quarter of a century. Trade with Europe was picking up once more. Vessels of every kind were sailing to Continental ports again. It was now perfectly feasible to journey across the Channel.

"By George, you're right!" Mr. Sandford declared. "Quick! We must go after them immediately! There is no time to lose! Take heart, madam! We may catch them yet!"

Denis Martin sprang to his feet. "We shall bring Roseanna home to you unmarried, Aunt," he promised.

He had already calculated that with a post chaise and fast horses they had a fair chance of overtaking Count Czarski.

Mr. Sandford had too.

"We shall pursue them even if they have taken a ship to the Continent!" he vowed.

"We shall indeed!" Denis seconded. "We'll stop them if we have to chase them into Poland itself!"

"You are not serious!" Evelina exclaimed. "You do not think Marek intends to go back there?"

"He may," Denis stated, shrugging. Then he sighed. "Yesterday I did not imagine Marek would elope with Roseanna. Today I see that anything is possible. It's a pity, really. If it weren't for that, I would have said he would make Roseanna an excellent husband."

"I cannot understand why you persist in defending him," Mrs. Poulet responded.

"He saved my life twice, Aunt," Denis answered sharply. "That's why."

Mrs. Poulet went even paler than she had been previously.

"What do you mean?" she inquired.

"Last year Marek saved the lives of hundreds of soldiers by stopping some French troops from massacring them when they were helpless and wounded in a hospital on the Continent," Denis replied. "I was one of them."

"And . . . and the second time?" Mrs. Poulet managed to ask.

"That was when he went over to France while he was on parole and ought not to have left England, so that he could rescue me yet again from Napoleon's rampaging army," Denis explained. "If he had been caught—by either side—it could have cost him his life."

Mrs. Poulet's eyes widened.

"Heavens!" she breathed.

"Marek also saved Roseanna's life," Denis informed her.

"What!" Mr. Sandford gasped. "I don't believe it!"

"This is the first I've heard of it!" Mrs. Poulet remarked skeptically.

"We didn't want to tell you," Denis said. "We thought you might be upset, and besides, Roseanna wanted us to keep it a secret. But now I feel you should know."

"So do I!" Mrs. Poulet exclaimed. "Pray enlighten me!"

"When did this happen?" Mr. Sandford queried.

"It was at the Frost Fair," Denis elaborated. "Roseanna was standing on a piece of ice that became detached from the main body and swept her down the Thames towards London Bridge."

Mrs. Poulet stifled a cry of horror.

"Marek was close by," Denis continued. "He jumped onto the ice with her and protected her. But for his quick action, she might have been swept off the ice into the water and have lost her life."

"Is this true?" Mrs. Poulet demanded of her niece.

"Yes, Aunt," Evelina answered.

Mrs. Poulet swayed where she sat. "Why wasn't I told earlier?" she asked.

"It is as Denis said," Evelina returned. "Roseanna didn't want you to know. She was afraid you would be too upset about it. And so were we. Since she was safe, there seemed no reason to worry you with it."

"I see," Mrs. Poulet murmured reflectively. "So he has some affection for her, has he? Well! That is a mercy, anyway!"

Denis Martin opened his mouth to speak, then shut it with a snap. Whatever redeeming qualities Count Czarski might have, he was still guilty of the enormity of eloping with Roseanna. And society, of which Denis was a member, found such a crime very hard to forgive.

Denis Martin and Mr. Sandford left North Row in a post chaise before breakfast. At every inn along the road to Dover they inquired about Roseanna and Count Czarski. At each place they halted to change horses they learned that a carriage with a couple answering the fugitives' description had been and gone an hour or so previously.

They arrived in Dover at eleven o'clock. Here they learned that the vehicle they had been pursuing had arrived at dawn. The man and woman in it had boarded a ship leaving on the early morning tide and were well on their way to the Continent.

"We have not missed them by much," Mr. Sandford

commented. "There's a merchantman leaving in an hour. If we sail on that, we'll not be far behind them."

"True," Denis agreed, "but they will have several hours' head start all the same."

"I know," Mr. Sandford responded. "However, I am sure we shall make it up once we are on land, especially if we have a good crossing, which we should, judging by the state of the sea at present. It looks beautifully calm!"

"No doubt," Denis remarked pessimistically, "but will it stay that way?"

"We'll soon see," Mr. Sandford replied cheerfully.

But, alas for his hopes, in a couple of hours the wind changed, and the crossing turned out to be a rough one. When the two men arrived in Calais they felt so ill that they decided they would have to rest in order to recover from their severe malady.

As soon as they were both better, they made further inquiries about the runaways. They learned that the two people they had been chasing after had indeed passed through Calais on their way to Brussels.

Immediately Mr. Sandford and Denis Martin set off in pursuit. In Brussels they learned that the miscreants had traveled on to Germany. However, as far as anyone knew, they had not been to a church.

"They are still unwed!" Mr. Sandford exclaimed with glee.

"We are in luck," Denis Martin agreed. "Now if only we can catch them before they see a priest!"

Onward the intrepid hunters journeyed, hiring horses at each stage of their trip and riding hard through Flanders into Germany. The trail, which had almost gone cold at Calais, was becoming warmer and warmer.

Since neither of the men spoke German, they had difficulty in explaining what it was they wanted. However, when they did finally make themselves understood, they received more news of the vehicle they were tracking down. Though they had lost an entire day through being tricked by Count Czarski and becoming seasick crossing the Channel, they had more than made it up. Early starts in the morning, fast mounts, and
178

their determination to keep going until it was too dark to see the roads had helped.

"They can't be far ahead of us now," Denis remarked.

"Yes," Mr. Sandford concurred. "We should catch them soon."

Denis Martin nodded in assent:

"And about time too!" he thought.

They had been on the road for four days. They were saddle-sore and weary.

Then, on the morning of the fifth day, they had word that the couple they were seeking were only two hours' ride ahead of them.

"Only two hours!" Denis echoed. "And Roseanna and Marek are still not married!"

Mr. Sandford was delighted. "We'll have them yet!" he breathed exultantly. "Before lunch we'll have them!"

They pressed onward, spurred to greater efforts by the promise of the victory which lay ahead.

"There they are!" Denis Martin exclaimed suddenly.

Mr. Sandford looked in the direction indicated.

"By Jove, you're right!" he cried.

Beneath them, at the bottom of a gently sloping hill, was the conveyance they wanted.

"Come on!" Mr. Sandford exhorted.

The men urged their horses forward, bearing down on the luckless vehicle. As they did so, it picked up speed.

Denis Martin drew out a loaded pistol and fired a warning shot.

The carriage shuddered to a halt. Within seconds Mr. Sandford and Denis Martin had drawn alongside it.

"Do you know," Roseanna commented when they stopped to admire the scenery on the second day of their flight, "it is funny, but I cannot conceive why we have not been followed."

"I am sure we must have been," Count Czarski stated.

"But we have seen nothing chasing after us, and we have been traveling relatively slowly. If someone pursued us on horseback, they would have caught up with us by now."

Count Czarski shrugged maddeningly.

"Are you sorry?" he questioned. "Would you like to be recaptured?"

"Oh, no!" Roseanna gasped in fright. "But . . ."

"But?" he prompted.

"I can't help thinking that if Mr. Sandford and Denis had been going to try to prevent us from marrying, they would have overtaken us by this time."

"I agree."

"And yet there has been no one running us down," she pointed out.

No wild cries of *"Stop! Stop!"* No carriages churning up the road as they raced after the fugitives. No sinister horsemen on the horizon.

As Roseanna finished speaking, she glanced at the count and saw that he had that same strange, quizzical expression in his eyes that she was beginning to recognize. He was up to some mischief or other. Or he was teasing her.

Hrmph! Well, that was a game two could play.

"Perhaps no one has missed me," she suggested.

"I can't credit that," Count Czarski responded. "Can you?"

Let's face it, she was not as good at this sort of thing as he.

"No. Not really." She hesitated before asking: "Marek, do you sincerely believe that Mr. Sandford and Denis have followed us?"

"Yes."

"But how? In a post chaise?"

"Perhaps."

"Then why haven't they caught us?"

"Why should they?"

Roseanna sighed with exasperation. "Because post chaises can drive very fast, and though we are in one during the day, we haven't been traveling at high speed," she informed him. "But they will."

"Maybe the gods are on our side," Count Czarski answered vaguely.

Roseanna decided that she could not stand any more of this.

"Marek!" she cried. "What is going on? Tell me! I must know!"

Count Czarski laughed. "Did you imagine I would leave anything to chance?" he inquired.

"I didn't have time to consider the question," Roseanna retorted. "If you will remember, we left North Row in rather a hurry."

Count Czarski smiled. "As soon as I received Evelina's note," he clarified, "I made plans so that we could get to safety in peace."

"Without being pursued?"

"Oh, no. It was inevitable that someone would try to catch us—probably Mr. Sandford—but I made allowances for that."

"What do you mean?"

"I hired some hackney carriages and a couple of acrobats from the circus, who resembled you and me from a distance, and paid them to act as decoys."

"I don't understand," Roseanna complained.

Patiently, Count Czarski explained how the acrobats, dressed in clothing similar to his own and Roseanna's, had been instructed to make use of the hackney carriages to lead any pursuers a merry dance, north, east, and west throughout London to the Oxford Street turnpike.

"If Mr. Sandford—and he is more likely to be the one than Denis—goes after them past Tyburn," Count Czarski concluded, "they will take him to Bath. Far, far away from us."

"Yes, I see," Roseanna murmured. "But what happens if he catches up with them before then?"

"He will find he has been deceived and that he has wasted precious time chasing them instead of us."

Roseanna laughed. "I'd like to see his face when he discovers!" she exclaimed.

"Yes. Pity we missed that."

"I suppose that will give us a couple of hours' head start," she reflected.

"Exactly."

"But what about when your little ruse is discovered?"

"My guess is that Mr. Sandford will be worn out from the exertion and angry because he was made to look like a fool. He will very probably return to North Row to discuss with your mother what he ought to do next."

"Hmmmmm. Yes. And then?"

Count Czarski shrugged. "They may retire for the night. Who knows?" he countered.

"Marek!"

"Perhaps someone will suggest that Mr. Sandford should go to the Albany to rouse Denis and seek his assistance."

"Do you want that?"

"Yes."

"Why?" Roseanna questioned. "Because it would create further delays?"

She reckoned that it would slow the pursuit down by another hour at the very least.

"Partly," Count Czarski concurred.

"Go on," Roseanna urged.

"Denis is not at his best during the early hours of the morning. His mind is rather fuddled—particularly if he has not had much sleep. I've noticed it on many occasions."

"You're not the only one," Roseanna commented. "He can be rather vague if he is overtired. But how will that help us?"

"If Mr. Sandford rouses Denis at, say, one o'clock in the morning," Count Czarski stated, "and tells him we have eloped, he will be shocked."

Roseanna nodded in agreement.

"The first thing he will do is look into my room to see if I am there or not," Count Czarski continued.

"And?"

"To throw him off the scent, I left him a note, saying I had gone to Portsmouth for a few days to supervise the building of the ship that is to take me to America."

"I don't understand."

"He will know that is not true. He will recall that

I told him last week that the ship was to be built in Rotterdam."

"Then why...?"

"I intended to make him angry, and by leaving that message I shall succeed."

"Oh, Marek! What ever for?"

"Because I know him. He will be determined to get me and he will join Mr. Sandford in endeavoring to hunt us down, which is exactly what I want him to do."

"You are joking!"

"No. I am perfectly serious."

"Explain!" Roseanna demanded.

"I have a plan, which depends on Denis being only half awake and also on his not knowing me as well as I know him."

Roseanna frowned. "When we were at the Frost Fair you told him he knew you well," she remarked.

Count Czarski nodded. "In some ways he does," he said. "But..."

A sudden terrible thought struck him. He had allowed for every contingency except one. His heart was in his mouth. It was only a little thing, but it was so important. His campaign depended on Denis Martin being unaware of one tiny detail.

But was he? Or had he by some mischance discovered Count Czarski's secret?

The couple in the conveyance clung to each other like a pair of frightened children.

"Please don't hurt us," they begged. "We don't have any money. We're poor people."

"It's not them," Denis Martin muttered.

"Cheer up," Mr. Sandford stated. "We have merely made a mistake and picked the wrong carriage. But they can't be far away."

The passengers exchanged glances.

"Have you, by any chance, followed us from London?" the man asked.

"Yes," Denis replied. "Why?"

"Are you Mr. Martin and Mr. Sandford?" the woman questioned.

"Ye-e-es," Mr. Sandford answered uneasily.

"In that case, we have a letter for you," the man informed him. "Would you mind very much signing for it?"

Impatiently Mr. Sandford and Denis put their signature to a slip of paper which, though they did not bother to read it, confirmed that the equipage had been stopped in Germany.

The couple inside hugged each other.

"Thank you," they said. "We'll get a bonus for coming this distance before we were caught. Good-bye."

Then they ordered their driver to turn around and head back to England.

Mr. Sandford and Denis Martin perused Count Czarski's note. As soon as they read it, they knew that he had intended this. He had bamboozled them into pursuing the wrong vehicle.

"I realize it is a little late for this, but," Count Czarski had written, *"April Fool."*

"What's the matter?" Roseanna queried as Count Czarski's face drained of color.

"You didn't tell Denis that I had English relatives, did you?" he asked.

"No," Roseanna answered. "I didn't tell anyone you were half English."

Count Czarski heaved a sigh of relief.

"Why should I do that?" Roseanna wondered.

Count Czarski shrugged, as was his habit when he did not wish to commit himself.

"Who knows?"

"Why is it important?"

"Because it is essential to my plan that Denis should not know," Count Czarski explained. "If he had found out, we ... we would have been done for."

"Well, *I* certainly didn't tell him."

"Good."

"Marek?" Roseanna pleaded.

Count Czarski understood her.

"Denis is aware that Poland is the only country I would care to visit in all Europe," he stated.

Once again Roseanna saw that flash of seering pain, and she knew that it hurt him deeply that he could no longer even visit the land of his birth without endangering his life.

"Being only half awake," Count Czarski continued,

"Denis will forget or ignore the fact that it is closed to me. He will conclude that since I sent the acrobats north, east, and west, but not south, that I must have gone south."

"Oh."

"My note informing him that I am on my way to Portsmouth will confirm his suspicions. He will realize that is another red herring. He knows that I cannot return to France, because of that escapade when I tricked the French authorities into handing him over to my custody. But he might accept that I would risk going through Calais if I were in a desperate enough hurry to leave England."

"Hmmmmm," Roseanna murmured as she considered this.

"Therefore," Count Czarski went on, "Denis will convince himself that not only have I gone south, but that I am heading for Poland."

"Yes, I see. So you think that he and Mr. Sandford will go south?"

"Definitely," Count Czarski responded. "They will pursue the carriage that I sent on ahead to the Continent. Its passengers are a man and a woman about our age. A nice couple, but poor. The woman reminded me of you. That's why I decided to give them the chance to improve their circumstances."

Roseanna blushed. "How . . . how did you find them?" she queried.

"I passed by as they were celebrating their wedding. I had just hired the acrobats, and seeing the happy pair come out of the church gave me another idea," he explained. "I asked them if they would like to earn a considerable sum of money. All they would have to do— and I assured them that was all . . . that there would be no tricks . . . nothing illegal—would be to go in a carriage as fast and as far as they could for as long as possible, directly into the heart of Europe, avoiding France except for Calais."

"And they agreed?"

"Of course. The adventure alone was worth it to them. Besides, I promised I would pay them twenty pounds to start with plus their expenses. In addition, my servants would drive them and assist them with any language difficulties."

"Your servants?" she inquired.

"Yes. I have more than one servant here in England," he replied. "Most of those who were loyal to me are exiles now. But only Tomasz stays at the Albany with me."

"Oh. I didn't realize."

Count Czarski smiled. "That's another thing Denis doesn't know," he stated.

"But didn't the newlyweds want to know the reason for this escapade?"

"Certainly."

"What did you tell them?"

"I said it was partly for a wager and partly for a little joke I was playing on Mr. Sandford and Mr. Martin. I gave them a note from me to deliver to those two if and when they caught up with them. I advised them to write the names of the towns they had passed through down on a slip of paper and to get Denis and Mr. Sandford to sign after the last one."

"Why?"

"It would stand as proof of how far they had gone, and for that I promised them a bonus of twenty pounds for each day beyond the first day they managed to hold up their pursuers. In addition, I shall give them a further twenty pounds if they go beyond the Dutch frontier."

Roseanna gasped. "But that is a fantastic sum!" she cried.

"Yes," Count Czarski concurred. "It was an offer they found too good to miss."

"So they accepted?"

"Yes."

"And Denis and Mr. Sandford are chasing after them instead of us?"

"I believe so."

Roseanna laughed aloud. "Oh, you are wicked, Marek!" she declared playfully. "How I wish Papa were alive! He would have enjoyed this so much!"

Count Czarski kissed her hands.

"How far do you think they will go?" Roseanna questioned, imagining Denis and Mr. Sandford chasing after the strangers halfway across Europe.

"Who knows?" Count Czarski countered. "Perhaps to Austria or Hungary. They might even see my country—if they are lucky."

Roseanna lowered her gaze. She had seen that sudden piercing shaft of pain in his eyes once more—that agony she never wanted to witness again for as long as she lived.

"Where are we going, Marek?" she asked him softly.

"Nowhere," he answered.

"Marek!" she scolded. "You are teasing me!"

"I am not."

"Yes you are!"

"No I'm not."

"But we must be going somewhere!"

"Really? Why?"

"Marek!"

He laughed at her failure to comprehend.

"My little darling," he murmured, "we have arrived."

"Arrived?" Roseanna echoed.

She looked around them, bewildered. There was nothing in view except for one or two tumbledown cottages and the undulating hills.

"Yes," Count Czarski confirmed.

"But . . . where are we?"

"In Gretna Green," he informed her. "That was why it was so important Denis did not know about my English relations. If he had discovered that, he might have deduced that I had brought you here."

"Oh," Roseanna responded, stunned.

"In a little while," Count Czarski told her, "we shall be married here."

Roseanna stared at him. "You mean," she inquired incredulously, "you sent Denis and Mr. Sandford all the way to the Continent and you have taken me just to Gretna Green?"

"That's right," he assented. "It is no use if they pursue us now. They'll be too far behind. If and when they catch up with us, we shall be man and wife."

Roseanna breathed a sigh of relief. To her, that meant that no one could separate them again.

"I'm so glad!" she exclaimed.

Count Czarski kissed her. "Come," he urged. "Let's see the parson and find out what conditions we have to comply with in order to be legally married."

Mr. Sandford gave a howl of fury. "We can still catch them!" he insisted. "If we return posthaste, we can still catch them!"

"No, we can't," Denis Martin contradicted.

"Why not?" Mr. Sandford demanded.

"For one thing, we don't know where they are," Denis pointed out. "If they are still in England, it will take us another four or five days simply to get back, and by that time Marek will have had nearly a fortnight in which to arrange to marry Roseanna."

"I ..."

"A special license. A trip to Gretna Green," Denis Martin enumerated. "There must be a hundred different ways of making her his lawful wedded wife. And yet you believe you can find Marek before he becomes Roseanna's husband?"

"Yes."

"All right. Where is he? Tell me that!"

Mr. Sandford swallowed. He could not conceive where the man had gone.

"I don't know," he admitted.

"I thought you wouldn't," Denis stated grimly.

"What do we do now?"

"There is nothing we can do except depart for North Row."

"Oh, no!" Mr. Sandford cried. He dreaded having to face Mrs. Poulet and confess that he had not managed to prevent this distasteful alliance. "I mean ... surely there is something we can do...."

"Such as?" Denis challenged.

Mr. Sandford shrugged. "I wondered if we might still ... stop them," he said lamely. "But there is no hope of that, is there?"

"No."

Mr. Sandford groaned.

"Don't despair," Denis exhorted. "It may be for the best. Who knows?"

Mr. Sandford ground his teeth.

"I cannot credit that," he responded.

Denis shrugged. "Shall we start back?" he inquired.

"Yes."

They rode for a while without speaking, and then suddenly an idea came to Mr. Sandford.

"All is not lost!" he declared.

Denis Martin smiled. "That's the spirit," he replied.

Mr. Sandford fell into a reverie. Despite what Denis Martin had told him when they were at the Albany and later, he believed the worst of Count Czarski. All at once, it occurred to him that it was possible that Roseanna might not have gone with Count Czarski willingly. In that case, any marriage could be annulled, and furthermore, Count Czarski stood to face criminal charges—kidnapping an heiress, no less!

"Let's see him charm his way out of that!" Mr. Sandford thought vengefully.

"So we are married now," Roseanna remarked as they journeyed southward into England.

"Yes," Count Czarski assured her. "Why? What's the matter? Don't you feel married?"

"I . . . I'm not sure," Roseanna answered hesitantly. "I suppose I am not used to it yet."

"Never mind," Count Czarski said. "When we are married for the second time, you will be more accustomed to it."

"Marek! You are teasing me again!"

"Am I?" he countered.

Roseanna regarded him quizzically. Was he? Or wasn't he?

"Aren't you?" she queried.

"No," he replied. "We shall have another wedding in less than a month, according to the rites and ceremonies of the Church of England. Then we shall return to London."

190

Roseanna frowned. "Why should we marry twice?" she asked.

"Can't you guess?"

"No."

"Are the men and women in England so different from those in Poland, then?"

"I don't follow you."

"Are there no talebearers in London? No busybodies? No scandalmongers?"

"Oh, yes. North Row is a hive of gossip. Everyone is so nosy. You can't put your head out of doors without the entire neighborhood knowing about it."

"Don't you see?"

"See what?"

"Think, Roseanna," he exhorted her. "Imagine your neighbors saying what a shame it was that you ran away with a foreigner and married at Gretna Green. How will your poor mother face them?"

"She won't like it, but . . ."

In a way she had brought it on herself. If she had not been so unreasonable . . .

"Don't you understand?" Count Czarski questioned. "It will sound so much better if she can tell them that we went north to meet my grandmother, *Lady* Nugent, and that our wedding was held at the estate of my cousin, *Lord* Telscombe, outside Brighton?"

Roseanna smiled. "You are right," she concurred.

"You agree to it, then?"

"Yes."

"Will that be enough for your mother?"

"What do you mean?"

"Scotland and England. We could always be married in Wales as well. And Ireland too, if necessary."

Roseanna had a horrifying vision of being dragged across the British Isles to go through wedding ceremony after wedding ceremony.

"No, no, Marek," she assured him hastily. "Twice will be enough . . . even for Mama!"

"Good," Count Czarski said. "Now there is only one thing I must ask of you."

"What is that?"

191

"In order for our second wedding to take place, we need your mother's consent . . . in writing."

"But how can we get that?"

"If you send her a letter via my servant, Tomasz . . ."

Roseanna froze. "But suppose she won't give us her permission?" she questioned apprehensively. "What if she . . . if she tries to part us?"

Count Czarski drew her close to him.

"She won't succeed," he stated firmly. "If she refuses to bless us, then she will be unable to separate us. I promise you."

"Oh. All right, then. I'll write to her."

"Excellent."

That evening they stopped at an inn in York, where they were to meet Count Czarski's grandmother. The good lady had not yet arrived, so Roseanna took the opportunity to compose a note to her mother, which she showed to the count when she had finished it.

"Very generous," he remarked when he finished reading the missive. "Let us hope she is as forgiving towards us."

"Yes," Roseanna murmured.

She had not considered it before, but now that she thought about it, a reconciliation would be nice.

Tomasz was summoned and given some commands in Polish by the count. He took the letter, clicked his heels, bowed, nodded in assent, and went on his way.

Roseanna gazed after Tomasz as he began his journey. When the servant was out of sight, she turned towards Count Czarski and saw that he was regarding her intently—almost frowning, in fact.

"What's the matter?" she inquired nervously.

"Nothing," he replied.

"You look cross."

Count Czarski smiled. "I was merely reflecting that we shall have a bed to sleep in tonight," he stated.

Roseanna blinked at him. She completely missed the implication behind his words.

"It is true," she mused. "We shall."

But why make an issue of it?

"I . . . I don't understand," she responded.

"Since we left London, we have been sleeping in the

carriage for the most part," Count Czarski commented. "And it was ... very bumpy."

"Oh," Roseanna said. "Yes."

He was quite correct. But what was the point?

Count Czarski appeared about to enlighten her, when his grandmother, Lady Nugent, arrived. Immediately he introduced the two women, and as he did so, he happened to remark that he had married Roseanna at Gretna Green.

At the mention of the place, Lady Nugent glared at her grandson. She insisted on treating Roseanna as Count Czarski's fiancée, rather than his wife.

However, though Lady Nugent ignored all reference to the Scottish border, she was obviously delighted with the prospect of having Roseanna as her granddaughter-in-law, and she began enthusiastically to discuss the second ceremony on Lord Telscombe's estate near Brighton.

Roseanna had been apprehensive of meeting Lady Nugent. However, she was soon at ease with the eccentric old lady and she enjoyed planning her wedding with her.

That evening, when Lady Nugent was occupied with something else, Count Czarski drew Roseanna aside and furtively put a key into her hand.

"What is this for?" Roseanna asked.

"The door," he answered mock-innocently.

"I don't understand."

"You've noticed how straitlaced Grandmother is?"

"Ye-e-es."

"You know that she refuses to accept that our marriage at Gretna Green is legal?"

"Yes. It is legal, though, isn't it?"

"Of course."

Roseanna heaved a sigh of relief. "Good," she murmured.

"I knew she wouldn't acknowledge the wedding at Gretna Green," Count Czarski stated. "She feels very strongly about it, though. She has even told the innkeeper to give us separate rooms."

"Oh."

Roseanna guessed that there was something important regarding this. But she could not comprehend what it was.

"I insisted that our rooms should be side by side, with a communicating door," Count Czarski informed her.

"Oh."

Still Roseanna was unaware what he was driving at.

"And this is the key to it," Count Czarski added.

Roseanna frowned. "Why are you giving it to me?" she inquired.

"In case you want it," he replied promptly.

"Why should I want it?" Roseanna wondered silently.

Count Czarski took her in his arms and kissed her very, very gently.

"We are man and wife now," he whispered. "If you need anything or want anything—anything at all—just unlock the door."

Roseanna's face cleared and she smiled.

"Yes, Marek," she responded, happy with the explanation. "Thank you."

It wasn't until later, when she was getting ready for bed, that Roseanna started to reconsider what Count Czarski had said to her concerning the key. It occurred to her then that there was a significance in the conversation which she had somehow missed.

"What did Marek mean?" she asked herself.

Why had he given her the key secretly? Why stress the fact of the communicating door? What was he endeavoring to tell her?

Roseanna's instincts warned her not to discuss the subject with anyone. She said nothing about it either to Lady Nugent, when she came in to bid her good night, or to the talkative, friendly maid who had entered to assist her to undress.

Eventually Roseanna was alone, with the main door to her room locked and bolted. She sighed as she
194

climbed into bed. Even though she had spent several minutes trying to work it out, she still did not understand what it was Count Czarski wanted.

"It must be important," Roseanna reflected, "or Marek would not have mentioned it."

There was only one way to find out. She slipped out of bed, took the key in her hand, blew out her candle, and, in the darkness, unlocked the door that separated her room from his.

Immediately before her, on the other side of the door, stood Count Czarski. Roseanna had a notion he had been waiting there for some time. She wondered fleetingly how long he would have remained there had she failed to appear just then.

Roseanna caught the briefest glimpse of Count Czarski's tense, bitter, set expression. However, the moment he saw her, his face changed. He smiled and held out his arms to her.

As Roseanna embraced him, she felt him crush her to him.

"I shall never regret unlocking that door," she thought. "Never as long as I live. Never, whatever happens!"

20

Mr. Sandford and Denis Martin made a sorry pair as they returned to London. The closer they came to the metropolis, the worse the situation had appeared to them.

"How are we going to break the news to Mrs. Poulet?" was the question uppermost in their minds, and: "How is she going to take it?"

They imagined the worst. A fit of hysterics. The doctor being summoned. Recriminations.

"Come on!" Denis urged, echoing Mr. Sandford's sentiments as they neared North Row. "Let's get it over with!"

Like lambs preparing for the slaughter, they went directly to Mrs. Poulet's house and knocked on the door. The maid admitted them to the drawing room, where they were warmly welcomed.

"Fancy you two coming back today!" Mrs. Poulet exclaimed.

"Yes, isn't it a coincidence!" Evelina cried.

Mr. Sandford and Denis Martin exchanged glances.

"It is the earliest we could make it," Mr. Sandford stated.

"Why?" Denis Martin questioned. "What is so special about today?"

"Nothing, merely that I have just received a letter from Roseanna," Mrs. Poulet informed them.

"What!" Mr. Sandford and Denis Martin gasped in unison.

"It was brought by hand," Mrs. Poulet added.

"Who brought it?" Denis wanted to know.

"Lord Czarski's Polish manservant," Mrs. Poulet replied.

"The one who doesn't speak English?" Denis queried.

"The same," Mrs. Poulet confirmed.

"He is waiting for an answer," Evelina said.

"Aha!" Mr. Sandford breathed significantly.

"What does she say, Aunt?" Denis Martin inquired.

"She writes that she and Lord Czarski went to Gretna Green, where they were married," Mrs. Poulet told them, grimacing.

"So my original guess was correct!" Mr. Sandford declared.

"It would seem so," Denis Martin agreed.

Mr. Sandford ground his teeth. If only he had heeded his instincts! He could have brought the pair of them back!

"Does she mention where she is writing from?" Evelina wondered.

"No," Mrs. Poulet responded. "But she says she hopes that we can still be friends, and that in time I will be able to accept Lord Czarski as her husband."

"Indeed!" Mr. Sandford exclaimed.

"It sounds like an extremely conciliatory letter," Evelina commented.

"In a way," Mrs. Poulet concurred.

"What do you mean, Aunt?" Denis questioned.

"Roseanna asks me to send my written consent to their wedding," Mrs. Poulet explained, "so that they can be married properly, according to the rites of the Church of England."

197

"Does she!" Evelina cried.

"I'll bet a pony that is Marek's doing!" Denis proclaimed.

"You are not going to give in to her, are you?" Mr. Sandford asked anxiously.

"Certainly not!" Mrs. Poulet snapped.

"You are going to refuse your permission?" Denis wanted to know.

"I am," Mrs. Poulet reiterated.

"Why?" Evelina queried.

"Because I do not approve of this Lord Czarski," Mrs. Poulet informed the company, "and I will not sanction his marriage to my daughter."

Evelina sighed. "But they are already married, Aunt," she pointed out. "The ceremony at Gretna Green was legal."

"I cannot accept that!" Mrs. Poulet insisted. "There must be a way of undoing the damage that wretch has caused."

"There is," Mr. Sandford said.

"Tell me!" Mrs. Poulet commanded.

"Write a reply to the letter," Mr. Sandford advised, "and give it to Lord Czarski's servant. You need not say you consent: Merely thank Roseanna for her note and state your reasons for not allowing them to marry."

"And then?" Mrs. Poulet inquired.

"We'll follow the man until he hands your letter to Roseanna," Mr. Sandford replied. "Then we shall be able to bring her back home to you."

"An excellent idea!" Mrs. Poulet enthused.

"And furthermore," Mr. Sandford continued, warming to his subject, "we'll have Lord Czarski arrested and charged with kidnapping her."

"Yes! Yes!" Mrs. Poulet agreed.

"Then," Mr. Sandford added, with relish, "the marriage shall be annulled and we can insure that they never see each other again."

"Is that possible?" Evelina questioned.

Denis Martin grimaced. "It is," he answered. He turned to the others. "Will it have to be done?"

"Of course it will have to be done!" Mr. Sandford exclaimed. "It is the only course of action open to us!"

"Is it?" Evelina challenged. "Why?"

"My dear young lady," Mr. Sandford responded patronizingly, "one cannot countenance elopements, can one? What would the world come to if everyone were to marry whomever they chose, regardless of what their parents felt was best?"

"I shudder to think!" Mrs. Poulet intoned, appalled by the notion.

"Hrmph!" Denis snorted. "Charging Marek with kidnapping Roseanna and having their marriage annulled seems a pretty poor way of repaying him for all he has done for me."

"Oh, Denis! Really!" Mrs. Poulet cried.

"He saved Denis's life twice," Evelina reminded them.

"He wiped out that debt by stealing Roseanna from her loving mama," Mr. Sandford retorted.

"Don't you agree?" Mrs. Poulet demanded.

"I suppose so," Denis murmured unhappily.

"What if Roseanna won't accuse Marek of having abducted her?" Evelina queried. "What if she says she went with him willingly?"

"She won't have that chance!" Mr. Sandford declared.

"I beg your pardon?" Evelina inquired.

"We shall not let him get to her this time," Mr. Sandford informed her.

Evelina raised her eyebrows superciliously.

"Do you intend to keep Roseanna a prisoner?" she questioned.

"Evelina!" Mrs. Poulet cried exasperatedly. "Of course not!"

"I am very sorry, but I am greatly puzzled by your attitude," Evelina apologized.

"I confess myself a bit baffled too, Aunt," Denis seconded. "I should be grateful if you would explain."

"Gladly!" Mrs. Poulet responded. "Roseanna, as you know, is a baby; a mere baby. She has no notion of what she has done. She is far too young to consider marrying. She is infatuated with Lord Czarski, nothing more. Once she has been home for a week or two, she

199

will forget him and there will be no more nonsense about this—ahem!—escapade!"

"Exactly. Lord Czarski will have no opportunity to bedazzle her again!" Mr. Sandford announced with satisfaction. "He will get what he so richly deserves!"

Evelina's eyes narrowed as she watched them. Although she was only a year older than Roseanna, in certain instances she was far more experienced in the ways of the world.

"Mr. Sandford and Aunt want revenge on Marek!" she thought.

It wasn't simply because Count Czarski was a Pole and had fought for Napoleon. Mrs. Poulet bitterly resented his having appeared on the scene and destroying her illusions regarding Denis Martin marrying Roseanna.

As for Mr. Sandford, he was smarting from the ignominy of having been tricked in the matter of the hackney carriages, not to mention having been hoodwinked into following strangers halfway across the Continent.

"Poor Roseanna!" Evelina reflected. "If they have their wish, it will break her heart!"

But what could she, Evelina, the poor relation, do about that?

Mr. Sandford and Mrs. Poulet were not going to be robbed of their chance to get even with Count Czarski. And Denis? Though he owed the count his life, he certainly did not approve of the elopement. At best, he was neutral.

"Poor Roseanna!" Evelina repeated silently.

She considered various ways of helping her cousin, but dismissed each of them. Then, when she had almost given up, it occurred to her that Roseanna's salvation lay with Count Czarski.

"Anyone clever enough and daring enough to sneak from England into war-torn France and whip Denis out from under the noses of his French jailors," Evelina told herself, "anyone sufficiently authoritative to prevent a massacre of wounded soldiers entirely on his own, is also probably possessed of the astuteness and the intelligence necessary to arrange a foolproof elopement."

In that case, Count Czarski knew what Roseanna had written to her mother. But why permit her to send the letter? Had he made plans concerning it? Had he, perhaps, forseen Mr. Sandford's and Mrs. Poulet's reaction?

"You don't suppose Marek is testing us, do you, Aunt?" Evelina asked.

"Testing us?" Mrs. Poulet echoed. "What ever do you mean, child?"

"He may have deduced that we are so angry that we are preparing to have him arrested and charged with kidnapping Roseanna," Evelina returned.

"Impossible!" Mr. Sandford exclaimed.

"Is it?" Evelina queried. "What if Marek suggested that Roseanna write to you, Aunt, so that he could show her just how far we will go? Suppose he sent his servant to us with her letter, knowing that someone would follow him? He could have made allowances for that, couldn't he?"

"Your imagination is running away with you, Evelina!" Mrs. Poulet cried.

"Definitely!" Mr. Sandford concurred.

"You don't think it is a probability?" Denis inquired.

"Absolutely not!" Mr. Sandford declared.

"Are you sure?" Evelina persisted.

"Positive!" Mrs. Poulet replied stoutly.

"The whole idea is complete rubbish!" Mr. Sandford contended.

"Is it?" Evelina demanded. "Remember, Marek has been one step ahead of you so far!"

"She is right there," Denis admitted ruefully.

Who would have believed that Count Czarski knew about Gretna Green? Who could have credited that he would take Roseanna there to be married instead of to the Continent?

"Don't you see what he is up to?" Mr. Sandford questioned.

"No," Evelina countered. "What?"

"He wants Mrs. Poulet to send her written consent

so that he can refute the kidnapping charge!" Mr. Sand
ford clarified.

"Hmmmmm. Ye-e-es," Evelina murmured.

She could see the reasoning behind that. It woul
be impossible for Mrs. Poulet to claim that her daugh
ter had been abducted by Count Czarski if he had
letter signed by her, giving her permission for Ro
seanna to marry the man.

And it confirmed what she had thought earlier
Count Czarski had anticipated this contingency.

"That is typical of him!" Mrs. Poulet declared. "H
should be punished for the unhappiness he has caused!"

"Precisely!" Mr. Sandford agreed. "I don't see wh
he should get away with what he has done!"

Denis frowned. "I don't follow you," he complained

"It is clear that Lord Czarski compelled Roseanna
to run away with him," Mr. Sandford explained, "t
marry him, and to write that letter."

"Really!" This was too much, even for Denis Martin
"Marek would never compel any woman to do some
thing against her will!"

"So you don't believe that he kidnapped Roseanna,
Evelina remarked.

"No, I don't!" Denis cried warmly.

"Would you be prepared to say so in court?" Evelina
wondered.

Denis started. "You are not serious!" he gasped.

"Aren't I?" Evelina questioned. "Haven't you been
listening?"

"Yes, of course, that is, I . . . er . . . well . . ." Denis re
turned.

"Mr. Sandford and Aunt propose to charge Marek
with forcibly abducting Roseanna," Evelina said mer
cilessly. "And you seem to imagine it won't come t
court!"

For a moment, Denis was speechless. He had no
realized the gravity of the situation. Then, as the truth
of her words dawned on him, he slumped into a chai
with his head in his hands. In a flash he saw the awfu
dilemma before him. Who should he side with? Hi
friend, to whom he owed his life twice over? Or hi
family?

"Oh, no!" he groaned.

"Denis," Mrs. Poulet probed anxiously, "you do agree with us that we must get the child away from him?"

Denis Martin shrugged helplessly.

"But what if Roseanna doesn't want to leave Marek?" Evelina mused. "What if she is miserable parted from him?"

"I wish you wouldn't indulge in these ridiculous speculations, Evelina," Mrs. Poulet snapped crossly.

"I am sorry, Aunt," Evelina began, "but I cannot help wondering if—"

"I have already told you," Mrs. Poulet interrupted. "Roseanna is a child. A mere baby. She may cry for him for a day or two, but she will soon recover."

Evelina raised her eyebrows skeptically. "I hope you are right, Aunt," she responded disbelievingly.

Denis looked even more worried than before.

"Do you think she really loves him?" he asked.

"Don't you?" Evelina countered.

"I don't know," Denis prevaricated.

"If she did not care for Marek, why did she leave with him?" Evelina demanded. "Why didn't she scream for assistance?"

"Maybe she did," Mr. Sandford suggested. "Maybe he overpowered her when she resisted him, and—"

"I told you Marek would never do such a thing!" Denis cut in angrily.

"You are not being very helpful, Denis," Mrs. Poulet stated silkily.

"I'm sorry," Denis Martin apologized.

"Just remember that Mrs. Poulet knows her daughter better than anyone else," Mr. Sandford said pompously. "As Roseanna's loving mother, she understands what the child's needs are."

"Hmmmmm. Er—ye-e-es," Denis concurred uneasily.

A silence fell. Only the ticking of the clock could be heard in the drawing room.

"Ahem!" Mr. Sandford remarked, breaking the hush by clearing his throat. "Are we agreed?"

"To do what?" Evelina queried.

Mrs. Poulet's eyes flashed furiously, warning he
niece to hold her tongue.

"Yes, we are. Pray proceed, Mr. Sandford," she in
vited him.

Mr. Sandford bowed slightly in acknowledegment.

"Mrs. Poulet will write a reply to Roseanna's lette
refusing her permission for this travesty of a union,
he proposed. "Denis Martin and myself shall follow
Lord Czarski's servant when he takes it to her. W
shall then do as I advised earlier."

"Any objections?" Mrs. Poulet wanted to know.

Evelina grimaced but made no response.

Denis Martin's expression was gloomy, but he to
refrained from speaking.

Mrs. Poulet took their silence for consent. She nod
ded with satisfaction and went to the escritoire to com
pose her missive.

"I shall be polite," she promised herself.

She was far calmer now than when she had firs
learned of the elopement. She was able to control her
self. She would say nothing offensive. But neithe
would there be anything to give so much as the meres
hint that she approved of what Count Czarski wa
doing.

"Roseanna's marriage at Gretna Green was nothin
more than a farce!" Mrs. Poulet reflected as she bega
to write. "My letter will convey that to her!"

21

Roseanna and Count Czarski continued to travel southward. They left York the day after Roseanna wrote to her mother and they journeyed in the direction of Brighton in easy stages, seeing as much of the countryside as they could during their circuitous journey, which was designed to avoid London.

Each night they stayed at an inn or a posting house in a town en route. And every time, Lady Nugent, Count Czarski's grandmother, was adamant that they should sleep in separate rooms.

Count Czarski never raised any objections. He appeared to acquiesce meekly. However, he always insisted that his room should have a communicating door with Roseanna's. The moment his grandmother's back was turned, he handed his wife the key to it. And Roseanna, who was beginning to know her husband, never failed to come to him.

"Not married?" Lord Telscombe questioned in surprise when their grandmother told him that Count Czarski and Roseanna would have to have separate rooms in his house. "Didn't you take advantage of Gretna Green, Marek?"

"Yes, we did," Count Czarski replied, "just like you two."

"Marek!" Lady Nugent declared. "Your cousin and his wife were married in the Church of St. Nicholas here on this estate, exactly as you and Roseanna will be! Gretna Green! I never heard of such a thing!"

Lord Telscombe, whose second wedding ceremony had followed his elopement to Gretna Green, looked askance. Lady Nugent was perfectly well aware of what occurred in his case. He glanced at Count Czarski, who merely shrugged.

Lord Telscombe decided to wait until he could speak to his cousin on his own.

"And what," he asked Count Czarski later, "was all that about?"

Count Czarski smiled. "Our dear grandmother refuses to acknowledge the legality of marriages contracted at Gretna Green," he answered. "As far as she is concerned, Roseanna and I are not man and wife, so we are to have separate rooms."

"You are surely not going to give in to the old battleaxe, are you?" Lord Telscombe demanded.

"Why not?"

Lord Telscombe was stunned. "Wh-why n-not?" he stuttered.

"If it makes her happy?"

Lord Telscombe made a choking sound. "If it—?" he gasped. "Marek! You are not serious!"

"Perfectly."

"Oh, Marek! Really! You—"

"I wouldn't upset our dear grandmother for the world," Count Czarski interrupted. "Just let us have two rooms with a communicating door, and hand the key of that over to me. There's a good fellow."

His final words were drowned by loud, vulgar laughter from his cousin.

Roseanna enjoyed her stay at Telscombe Park. She liked Count Czarski's cousins and she was happy to spend her days making plans for the wedding, which Lady Nugent seemed determined was to be a grand affair.

However, she was not entirely easy in her mind.

"Marek," she murmured, one night when they lay in bed together.

"Yes?" Count Czarski queried.

"What if Mama won't let us marry?"

"Don't worry about that now."

"I can't help it. Please, Marek. What happens if she refuses her consent?"

Count Czarski lifted his shoulders.

"Grandmother will be horribly disappointed," he stated.

"Marek!"

"We could go over to Flanders and have our second wedding ceremony over there," he answered. "Or Holland. Or wait until we arrive in America. It shouldn't make very much difference."

"But..." Roseanna began.

She paused and bit her lip uncertainly.

"What is it?" Count Czarski questioned gently. "What is troubling you?"

"You remember that letter you wanted me to write and which Tomasz was going to take to Mama?"

"I remember."

"Well, suppose Mr. Sandford and Denis decide to follow Tomasz here," Roseanna stated, "and they find us, and—"

Count Czarski laid his finger on her lips, silencing her.

"They will never manage to do that," he assured her.

"Why not?"

"Because they won't," he said firmly.

Roseanna grimaced. "But why not, Marek?" she persisted.

Count Czarski sighed. "All right! All right! I'll explain it to you!" he exclaimed. "Then will you stop worrying?"

"That depends," Roseanna prevaricated.

"On what?"

"On what you tell me," Roseanna informed him coyly.

Count Czarski smiled. "Ah, yes," he murmured, and started to kiss her, "doesn't it, though?"

Several minutes elapsed before Count Czarski spoke again.

"Before Tomasz left the inn where we were staying in York," he remarked, "I gave him detailed instructions."

"Was that when you talked to him for so long?" Roseanna asked.

"Yes. I directed him to take your letter to your mother in North Row and to wait for her reply. When she had given it to him, he was to take it to the nearest posthouse on the Great North Road, where he would remain overnight."

"I don't follow."

"Patience, my love," Count Czarski admonished. "You will."

"Go on, then," Roseanna urged.

"When Tomasz is safely locked in his room," Count Czarski continued, "he is to write our address here at Telscombe Park on the envelope of the note your mother has given him. This he will hide in his coat pocket. Then he is to take a second envelope, which, let me assure you, will be exactly like your mother's, and carry it openly in his hand when he leaves the posthouse next morning."

"I still don't understand," Roseanna complained.

"That is because you are still being impatient," Count Czarski chided.

"Oh. Sorry. What then?"

"Tomasz will travel by post chaise to York," Count Czarski went on. "Either that night or some time during the day, as soon as he can do so without being observed, he is to send your mother's letter here to us."

Roseanna frowned. "And?" she prompted.

"He is to do this secretly, so that no one chasing

after us will realize what he is up to," Count Czarski elaborated.

"Can he? I mean, he looks such a simple soul, and this sounds like a complicated plan."

Count Czarski smiled. "Tomasz may be old, but he is no fool," he informed her. "He is used to carrying secret messages. Believe me, for Tomasz this will be nothing new."

"Oh."

"Can I go on?"

"Yes please."

"Since Tomasz will still be carrying in his hand a letter that resembles the one your mother wrote to you, anyone in pursuit should be convinced that he is to deliver it to you in person—"

"—and they will follow Tomasz to York!" Roseanna exclaimed, suddenly seeing the light.

"That's right."

"But what good will that do?"

"If your mother has given us her permission to marry, my plans won't be necessary. Tomasz will have had a long journey for no purpose, because if she has forgiven us, then no one will follow him."

"Oh. But what if she has withheld her consent?"

"In that case, the letter we receive will be cold and disapproving. She will say that under no circumstances will she countenance our marrying. Furthermore, she will send Mr. Sandford and probably Denis as well to pursue Tomasz in the belief that he will lead them to you."

"Why?"

"If your mother is set against us, my love," Count Czarski explained, "she will want to separate us."

"Can she do so, now that we are married?"

"Yes."

"H-how?"

"If the letter had been sent by hand directly to us, she might have succeeded."

"But—"

"Imagine we were still at that inn in York, and Tomasz arrived with the letter, which he handed to you

209

and which contained your mother's refusal to allow us to marry."

"Very well."

"Suppose that Mr. Sandford and perhaps Denis too came hot on Tomasz's heels. They would find you reading the letter and they would insist on taking you back to London—by force if necessary."

Roseanna shuddered.

"In the rumpus that followed," Count Czarski continued, "they would charge me with kidnapping you and Tomasz with being an accessory. We should both be arrested and thus unable to stop your return to North Row. Once there, you would undoubtedly be kept locked in your room until I had been tried and convicted—"

"Oh, Marek, they couldn't! No court in the land would—"

"Yes, they could, and they would," Count Czarski interrupted. "You see, *I* paid for our expenses on that trip, so there is no evidence to show that you came willingly."

"They would judge it on that?"

"Yes."

"But that is—"

"Ridiculous?" he suggested.

"Definitely."

Count Czarski shrugged once more. "After I had been sentenced," he concluded, "they would have our marriage annulled."

Roseanna trembled.

"I'm sorry," he murmured. "I didn't mean to upset you."

"It's all right," she whispered. "But what happens now?"

"That depends on what your mother writes," he replied. "We are quite safe, whatever her decision."

"How? What if she won't consent? What could we do?"

"By going to York with the false letter in his hand, Tomasz will give us time," Count Czarski explained. "If your mother has turned us down, we will know well before Mr. Sandford or Denis discover my little ruse."

"And then?"

"We pack our things and leave England as soon as we can."

"Oh."

Count Czarski caressed her. "Cheer up," he said. "She may give us her blessing."

Roseanna smiled at the thought. "I hope she does," she stated.

"Hmmmmm. So do I."

"Marek?"

"Yes?"

"What about Tomasz?" Roseanna questioned. "What will happen to him once he reaches York?"

"Nothing."

"Come on, Marek!"

"Whether Tomasz finds he is being followed or not, as soon as he arrives in York he is to turn round and make his way to Holland. He will meet us in Rotterdam, where our ship is. Whatever happens, we shall all sail from there very soon."

"All?" Roseanna echoed.

"Yes, all."

"Who is all?"

"The other servants I told you about. And grandmother is coming with us."

"What!"

"Didn't I mention that?"

"No. You didn't."

"Sorry. It slipped my mind."

Roseanna gave him an old-fashioned look.

"Is she going to live with us?" she wanted to know.

"Not exactly."

"What does that mean?"

"Grandmother is going to live near us, but she will have her own living quarters so that she can be independent. Satisfied?"

"Yes. I think that is a good idea."

"Are you happy now?" he demanded. "Have you stopped worrying?"

"Yes," Roseanna answered, and curled up in his arms.

Evelina watched as her aunt began to draft her missive. She knew that Mrs. Poulet intended to be scathing and disparaging about Roseanna's elopement with Count Czarski. Her instincts informed her that Roseanna's mother would regret doing anything to try to break up the couple. But how could she make her aunt see that?

"Aunt," she inquired, "may I ask you a question?"

Mrs. Poulet stopped writing. "Of course, dear," she replied. "What is it?"

"I hope you won't think badly of me for suggesting this, Aunt," Evelina started nervously.

Mrs. Poulet frowned. "Why should I do that, dear?" she wondered.

"Well, you might feel I was being forward or . . . rude," Evelina responded.

Mrs. Poulet's frown deepened. "Indeed?" she queried.

"Ummmmm," Evelina murmured, sweeping the carpet with one foot.

"Evelina, for heaven's sake say what you want to say and get it over with!" Mrs. Poulet ordered. "You know how I abhor people who dither!"

"What if Roseanna is pregnant?"

There was an appalled silence following Evelina's words. Mrs. Poulet became a shade paler. Mr. Sandford and Denis Martin went bright red.

Mrs. Poulet recovered her voice first.

"Evelina!" she cried. "How could you?"

"I am sorry, Aunt," Evelina apologized contritely. "But I couldn't help considering whether—"

"Impossible!" Mrs. Poulet cut in. "Roseanna wouldn't! She has been far too well brought up!"

"Precisely," Mr. Sandford agreed. "I am amazed that you can entertain such a notion!"

"If Roseanna heard you," Denis stated, "she would probably die of shock."

"I doubt it," Evelina remarked dryly.

"She would hardly thank you for your opinion!" Mrs. Poulet commented.

Evelina shrugged maddeningly.

"Your cousin would never permit a strange man to—er—to take advantage of her!" Mr. Sandford declared.

"Marek isn't a strange man," Evelina pointed out.

"Yes he is!" Mrs. Poulet insisted.

"Of course he is," Mr. Sandford concurred. "They have not known each other for more than a few weeks!"

"In her letter Roseanna told us that he is her husband," Evelina reminded them.

"Fiddle faddle!" Mrs. Poulet exclaimed. "That marriage is no more than a sham!"

"Quite," Mr. Sandford seconded. "Lord Czarski her husband? Balderdash!"

"Is it?" Evelina mused.

"Certainly," Mrs. Poulet returned.

"And do you sincerely imagine that is what Marek believes?" Evelina questioned.

Denis Martin gasped. "You're right!" he cried.

"What are you talking about, dear boy?" Mrs. Poulet inquired.

"If Roseanna feels the marriage in Gretna Green was legal, then so does Marek," Denis informed everyone. "And—forgive me for saying so, Aunt—but he is not monkish by any means!"

"He . . . he will make her his . . . his *real* wife?" Mr. Sandford croaked.

"Undoubtedly," Denis replied.

Mrs. Poulet and Mr. Sandford were nonplussed.

"Oh, Lord!" Denis continued. "Aunt, I am afraid we must consider the possibility that he and she . . . that— er . . . Well, she did write in her letter that they were man and wife!"

Mrs. Poulet stared at the others. She read in their expressions that she was beaten.

Mrs. Poulet took the letter she had begun to write and tore it to shreds.

"I shall have to draft a fresh one," she thought, "giving them my blessing."

If she wanted to see her beloved daughter again, nothing less would do.

22

"It is a pity that Mama could not see this," Roseanna whispered to Count Czarski as they walked down the aisle together.

"Yes, it is," Count Czarski agreed. "You did send her an invitation, didn't you?"

"Of course. Evelina says that she thanked me but that she could not come because she had a terrible migraine."

"Does she blame me?"

"Oh, no! She couldn't possibly do that!"

Then they stepped out of the cool interior of the church into brilliant sunshine and Count Czarski and Roseanna smiled at the crowd of people who had gathered in the churchyard to wish them well.

By the time Roseanna and Count Czarski returned to London, the neighbors in North Row had heard all about their marriage. The story Count Czarski had
214

devised, and which was the one Roseanna's relations had adopted, was that Roseanna and he had traveled to York to meet his grandmother, and that the three of them had then journeyed to Telscombe Park for the wedding. Fortunately, it was so plausible that the notorious gossips of North Row never suspected there was more to it than that. Society was impressed. Those who had heard vague rumors about the wedding at Gretna Green were prepared to ignore them.

Mrs. Poulet was reconciled to Roseanna's marriage to Count Czarski—almost. She delighted in telling her acquaintances that Roseanna was a countess and intimated that the idea that she should marry Count Czarski was in reality hers.

The arrival of Lady Nugent's carriage, with her ladyship, Count Czarski, and Roseanna in it, had the neighbors peering out from behind their curtains.

"She hasn't changed!" Mrs. Poulet cried as she caught sight of her prodigal daughter.

She rushed down the path, kissed Roseanna, hugged Count Czarski, and embraced Lady Nugent. No one seeing the warmth of her welcome could credit that there had been any opposition to the match.

"Roseanna!" Evelina greeted her cousin. "What a lovely gown!"

White French muslin figured with orange flowers. Very becoming. Very expensive, too.

"You like it?" Roseanna asked as they walked into the drawing room.

"Yes. Very much. What did it cost?"

"I don't know. Marek had it made for me, but he wouldn't tell me the price."

Evelina's response was lost in the babble of voices as the other members of the tea party entered the drawing room and took their places.

"Such a pity you couldn't come to the wedding," Lady Nugent was heard to remark above the hubbub. "We were so sorry, Mrs. Poulet, that you were not present."

"Yes, so were we," Evelina answered for her relation, "but Aunt had an excruciating migraine. It quite broke my heart to see her in such agony."

215

"Yes, it was truly the worst I have ever suffered," Mrs. Poulet added.

"What a shame!" Lady Nugent exclaimed. "It was a delightful affair!"

"Do tell me about it," Mrs. Poulet requested.

The conversation then turned on the preparations for the wedding and the great day itself, and from there it progressed on to the count's plans to leave for America.

"So you really are going to go there, Marek," Denis Martin stated.

"Yes," Count Czarski confirmed.

"When do you sail?" Mr. Sandford wanted to know.

"Soon," Count Czarski responded. "We have some minor adjustments to make, but it won't be long now."

"Will you be staying in London?" Evelina questioned Lady Nugent politely.

"Yes," Lady Nugent replied, "for a couple of days, at any rate."

"A couple of days?" Denis repeated. "Where are you going after that?"

"We intend to leave for Holland before the end of the week," Lady Nugent informed him.

"Before the end of the week!" Mr. Sandford echoed.

"I did say *soon*," Count Czarski reminded him.

"But you cannot leave just now!" Mrs. Poulet declared.

Count Czarski did not answer her. Instead he gazed into his teacup. Then, seeming to realize it was empty, he put it on the table and abruptly rose to his feet.

"There is no reason for us to stay on," Lady Nugent commented. "We have settled our affairs and there is nothing further to keep us in England."

"Roseanna, is this true?" Mrs. Poulet demanded.

"I'm afraid so, Mama."

By now Count Czarski had come to rest behind Roseanna's chair.

"Why don't you join us on our trip, madam?" he suggested.

"What?" Mrs. Poulet queried.

"Come to America with us, Mama," Roseanna clarified.

"Oh, no!" Mrs. Poulet exclaimed. "I couldn't possibly."

"Well, come with us to Holland and see us off, then," Lady Nugent invited.

But Mrs. Poulet hardly heard her.

"Roseanna," she said enticingly, "you can't leave now. You'll miss all the fun."

Roseanna was interested. "What fun?" she asked.

"The victory celebrations," Mrs. Poulet answered. "Everything is going on. Do stay longer!"

"Everything?" Roseanna inquired. "Such as?"

"The Proclamation of Peace procession, the parties, the fireworks," Mrs. Poulet enumerated seductively, "the balls, the illuminations..."

"...not to mention the foreign dignitaries," Evelina added.

Roseanna's brow wrinkled. "Foreign dignitaries?" she questioned. "Who, for instance?"

"The King of Prussia is coming to London soon," Denis tempted her. "The Prince of Orange is already here, and there is speculation that he may marry Princess Charlotte before the summer is out."

"Wouldn't you like to see that?" Mr. Sandford wondered.

"Well-ll-ll..." Roseanna prevaricated.

In the back of her mind was the nagging suspicion that Count Czarski had deliberately evaded discussing the subject with her. But why?

"Perhaps I am imagining it," she mused silently.

Then she recalled how, earlier that year, she had had the distinct impression that Count Czarski had purposefully shunned social events at which the Prince Regent was present. She remembered that at the time she had been unable to discover a reason for his doing so, and therefore she had dismissed the notion. And yet...

"As far as I can tell, we are about to receive a whole galaxy of European royalty," Evelina stated, "of whom the King of Prussia and the Prince of Orange are but two."

"Really?" Roseanna's curiosity was aroused. "Who else?"

217

"Prince Metternich, the Prince of Bavaria, the Prince of Coburg, Prince William, Prince Augustus and Prince Henry of Prussia, the Prince of Württemberg," Evelina began, "the Duc d'Orléans, the Duke of Saxe-Weimar..."

"...and," Mrs. Poulet breathed ecstatically, "the Czar of Russia is coming here on the sixth of June. Think of that!"

As Count Czarski was standing behind her, surveying the company, Roseanna could not see him wince, but she knew that he must have done so.

"He knows," Roseanna reflected. "That is why he made Grandmother settle her affairs so swiftly."

He did not want to come across the Czar—ever.

"That also explains why he wants to leave England so quickly," Roseanna thought. "If the Czar ever learns that he is in this country, he could well insist that Marek be sent to Russia—to face trial for treason!"

Suddenly it dawned on her. Her instincts had been correct. Count Czarski *had* been avoiding making a name for himself in society. If he had been noticed... if word of his whereabouts had reached the Kremlin...

"I would have lost him!" Roseanna realized.

If Count Czarski were not deported, he would be murdered by the Czar's secret police.

Roseanna froze. A split second was sufficient for her to consider what she ought to do.

"No, Mama," she said firmly. "I think not."

Count Czarski snatched her hand and kissed it fervently.

Tears pricked Roseanna's eyes. So that was why he had not told her! He trusted her to know better than to consent to remain in England.

Roseanna controlled her trembling lip. She understood her husband well enough by now. It was not only the Foreign Office decree condemning him to the Czar's tender mercies that he feared. He had escaped before— he might do so again.

"He is afraid that he will not be able to restrain himself," Roseanna mused, "in the presence of the monster who is responsible for the slaughter of so many of his dear ones."

Better that they should leave the country now and miss the victory celebrations than risk that!

"But Roseanna—" Mrs. Poulet began.

Roseanna did not let her finish.

"No, Mama," she interrupted quietly but decisively.

In an instant, Mrs. Poulet realized that she had been wrong earlier in assuming that Roseanna had not changed. She had. Imperceptibly, in the last few weeks, she had grown up.

"I ..." she started uncertainly. "Oh, well, perhaps we'll come to Holland to see the three of you off there. How do you feel about that, Mr. Sandford?"

"An excellent idea!" Mr. Sandford declared. "May I have the honor of escorting you, madam?"

"Of course," Mrs. Poulet murmured.

"What about you, Denis?" Count Czarski questioned. "Are you going to see us off too?"

"I wouldn't miss it for the world," Denis Martin returned.

"How nice!" Lady Nugent exclaimed. "We shall be delighted to have you all, won't we, Marek?"

"Yes indeed," Count Czarski agreed. "Are you sure you would not like to emigrate with us?"

"Quite sure," Mrs. Poulet, to whom the invitation had been extended, responded hurriedly. "England is my home. I ... I would not be happy anywhere else."

"If ever you change your mind, Mama ..."

Roseanna did not have to complete her sentence. Mrs. Poulet smiled in understanding.

The ship floated alongside the dock. The final preparations had been completed at last. The servants hurried on board. The crew were already busy with their duties. Lady Nugent, Roseanna, and Count Czarski were saying farewell to those who had come to see them off.

Then the ropes were cut loose, the anchor was hoisted, the sails filled, and the vessel began to glide toward the open sea. Roseanna, Count Czarski, and Lady Nugent stood on deck, waving to those they were leaving behind, until they disappeared from view.

They had started to sail in the morning, in order to cover as much of the Channel as they could before nightfall, when the waters were not as safe as everyone might wish. Those who were good sailors like Roseanna remained on deck, gazing at the ever-changing coastline and admiring the beauty of the sun and sea.

It was evening and the light had faded before everyone finally retired to their cabins. By then there was a fresh breeze and the ship rolled rhythmically in time to the waves. It was not much of a roll, but as Roseanna was unaccustomed to it, it took her longer than usual to undress.

When Roseanna emerged from the dressing room and entered their cabin, she found that Count Czarski was already waiting for her. He was reclining on the bunk, and as she walked past him toward the mirror, intending to do her hair, he handed her a slip of paper.

"What is this?" Roseanna asked without looking at it.

"Don't you recognize it?" Count Czarski questioned.

"No. Ought I to?"

"You might."

"Well, I don't. What is it?"

"The letter you wrote to me before we were married."

Roseanna went cold. "I see," she responded unenthusiastically.

"You don't approve of it?"

"No."

"You should, you know."

"Why?"

"It has been very useful to us."

"In what way?"

"It was that letter which I gave to Tomasz to use as a decoy in case your mother's reply to our request for her permission to marry was a refusal."

"Oh."

"Aren't you going to read it?"

Roseanna eyed him apprehensively.

"You think I should?" she inquired.

"Yes. Why not?"

Unwillingly, Roseanna unfolded the missive and

perused it. As she studied the words her mother had dictated, she gave an angry gasp.

"What a horrible letter!" she exclaimed. "You should have burned it, Marek!"

"Burned it?" he questioned teasingly. "Why? Isn't it true?"

"You know very well it isn't true!" Roseanna retorted crossly. "It must be burned!"

Count Czarski shrugged indifferently.

"Burn it if you wish to," he answered.

Roseanna did not wait to be asked twice. She struck a match and set fire to the note. She was careful to insure that the flames were contained, however, so that nothing in the wooden vessel in which they were traveling could possibly catch fire.

As the paper was transformed into a mass of charred ashes, Count Czarski sighed forlornly.

"Pity!" he murmured.

Roseanna directed her attention to her hair, which he had prevented her from brushing when she had first entered their cabin. She had her back to him, so she could not see his face as she replied.

"Marek!" she declared. "You surely did not want to keep that, did you?"

"It would have made a nice souvenir," he remarked, "in a way."

Roseanna frowned. "In what way?" she questioned.

"I felt it might amuse our grandchildren."

Roseanna continued to do her hair. Grandchildren? What was he talking about? They didn't have any children yet, let alone grandchildren!

Roseanna veered round to look at him. He was stretched full-length on their bunk, gazing at her with an expression that was at once wistful, amused, and pleading.

"Don't you think you've put the cart before the horse, Marek?" she queried.

"What do you mean?" he countered innocently.

"You have to have children before you can have grandchildren," she pointed out.

Count Czarski became very pensive.

"Yes, you do," he reflected solemnly. "Don't you?"

Roseanna's brows drew together. She went on brushing her hair while she tried to work out the significance of the odd note in his voice. Presently she rose from her place.

"What is he up to now?" she wondered as she tidied the ashes of her note away.

She walked across the carpet, which he had had laid in their cabin so that she, who never wore slippers, would not get cold feet, and stood in the center of the room surveying him. He was still reclining on the bunk, but his eyes were cast down, instead of looking straight at her as they usually did.

If he had been a woman, Roseanna would have concluded that he was being either demure or coy. Or was he trying to conceal something?

"It takes time...to...to have children," she commented.

"We'll have quite a bit of time on this voyage," he told her casually.

Roseanna's eyes widened as the penny dropped.

"Marek!" she exclaimed, coming toward him.

"Yes?" he queried.

"Why can't you ever ask me for that simply? Why do you have to use such roundabout methods?"

Count Czarski's lips twisted into that enigmatic smile she was beginning to know well.

"I do so love seeing how long it takes you to get it," he murmured contritely.

"Naughty!" she scolded, sinking into his outstretched arms.

"Am I?"

"Yes—and you know it."

"Tsk. Tsk. Shame on me, then."

Roseanna sighed. It was useless taking her husband to task. Ever since they had first met he had been like that. The hints he had dropped! And she had not had a clue as to what he had been referring to! Looking back, though...

"One of these days," she threatened, "I might pretend I don't understand at all, and then you'll be sorry."

Suddenly that flash of searing pain appeared in his

eyes, and along with it, though Count Czarski made no move, Roseanna sensed an underlying tension.

It was incredibly brief. Count Czarski brought himself under control in an instant. No stranger would even have been aware of it.

But Roseanna noticed.

"I was only teasing, Marek," she said softly. "I didn't mean it."

As she spoke, she caressed him lovingly. Her lips brushed his and she felt him relax once more. Then he responded to her....